Run, Run, Baby

GITTE TAMAR

BTW LLC

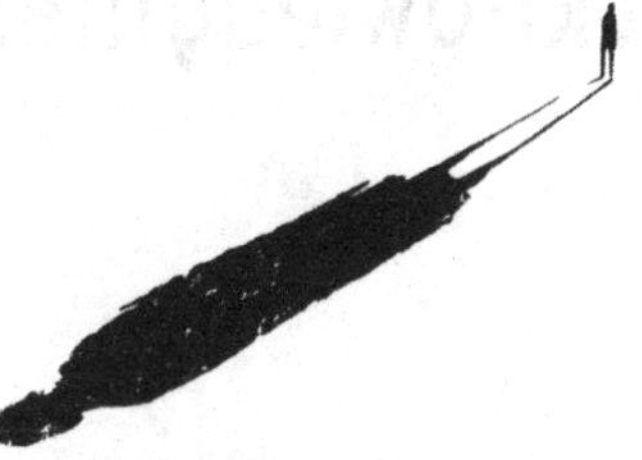

Those tortured by bullying peers never forget the resilience gained through each depressive fit of monumental tears.

Acknowledgment

Thank you to each of my family and friends, you already know who you are, so I will refrain from listing each of your specific names. Just know I will forever be thankful for each one of you who provided me with never-ending troves of love and emotional support.

Thank you to all of my readers for continuing to embark on this journey with me. I am forever indebted to you.

Contents

Chapter One

THE CLOCK MONSTER

As the loud air conditioning unit blasts into the kindergarten class, a tunnel of wind forcefully weaves between each of the crusted window frame blinds. The swift movement of the airflow induces a low-grade hissing sound that mimics a sea serpent sneaking up on its prey.

Children's finger paintings that highlight what each child is thankful for hang in a row next to the forest-green chalkboard on the off-white wall. Eerie darkness drowns each elementary student's handprint drawings of turkeys, and the happy splattering of vibrant colors takes on a melancholy tone. The rusted thumbtacks that hold the darkened portraits onto the classroom wall reek with smells of deep iron.

A small ray of light escapes through a window blind to give a glimpse of a six-year-old girl's small blue eyes surrounded by dark rings. Sitting at a single wooden desk in the middle of the classroom, her eyes dart to a circle of empty green chairs that surround her, and she becomes paranoid. As the Invisible bodies stare back at her, a terrible fear that something is coming grows in her gut.

The small chunk of light moves across the meek child's frame as she nervously fidgets in her seat, and her frantic nature displays her tragic attire. Her sunken cheeks describe one of the dark monsters that haunt her waking life, and the signs of malnutrition on her petite frame are exaggerated by the dirty blonde hair that highlights the color of the dark purple stains under her eyes.

Trying to comfort her mind, Chloe hums an oddly cynical melody that seems unsuitable for a child. Running her cold fingertips through the moth-bitten holes in her dress, she desperately scans the room to look for an escape.

During her final glances at the room's exit points, she hears the ticking of a large circular clock mocking her. With every second that passes, the click of the Gothic hands grows louder, and the abrupt sound of small jabs feeds into Chloe's deep-seated fears of her life running out of time.

Tick, tick, tick, tick, the clock counts.

Ending her bout of humming, she listens closely to what the school clock is saying. Instead of protecting the child, the ticking tone invites a dark entity to join them, and the anticipation of the familiar visitor creates a twitch in her eye. Attempting to take control of the situation, she closes her eyes tightly and resumes humming the original melody at a quicker pace.

Tick, tick, tick, laughs the clock as it grows louder to mock her attempt.

In desperation to stop the scene from escalating, Chloe taps her pencil to the beat of each tormenting click.

"I'm dreaming. Just wake up, Chloe. Wake up," she whispers to herself.

Beating her pencil louder against the desk's slivered wood, her hand becomes frozen and unable to move. Opening her eyes, she looks for the cause of her hand's immobility, and her curiosity turns to horror.

Possessed by the dark entity, her hand holding the pencil abruptly twists and uncontrollably scribbles on the desk. The harsh jerking movement creates a sound like a breaking twig as her frail bone pierces through her wrist's delicate skin. The friction from the violent shading of the wooden pencil rubs her fingers raw to the point of bleeding, and the red hue with the black lead creates a more explicit depiction of her worst nightmare.

"Chloe..." a raspy voice calls from the shadowy edge of the torturous clock. As the picture nears completion, the haunting creature's plan comes to fruition, and the pain from the repetitive jolts of her wrist becomes unbearable as tiny hairline fractures form on her exposed bone.

Waterfalls of tears tumble from Chloe's swollen red eyes and smudge the lead-ink portrait etched into her desk. She considers herself powerless, as any hope that she had previously mustered is ripped from her haphazardly beating heart.

"Chloe, Chloe, Chloe..." The gruff voice echoes louder. The voice gains power and continues to escalate in volume as it feeds off her exuding fear.

Releasing the pencil from her cramping fingers, she watches as it tumbles to the dirty vinyl floor. Staring at the finished etching causes her pupils to resemble a total eclipse and turbulent shivers to play hopscotch down her spine. The presumptuous scale of dark-shaded lines with cherry hues manifests a long, skinny, shadowy figure that her innocent mind finds uncomfortably familiar.

Her features begin to melt as her heart races past the tipping point of distress, and, opening her mouth to scream, her lips become tacky, like hot glue. Like a jailbird in a cage, the sticky skin blocks her cries for help, and she considers her body trapped like a prisoner on death row.

"Chloe..." the listening voice shouts with more precise diction.

Panicking, she looks to the only exit, and her heart shrinks in her chest as the room stretches taller. Wanting to escape before the creature devours her soul, she tries to stand on her lethargic feet to run, but she is rooted to the spot like an insect caught on a sheet of flypaper.

Pain exudes from each finger as the tips liquefy like hot wax onto the wooden desk and combine with the dark-laced drawing. As the skin re-hardens, lead seeps into the crevasses of her exposed wounds and paints the visible white bone from her wrist the color of brick red.

Convinced that her life is ending, she tries to scream through her gummy lips, and the predicted muffled pleas for help add to her pain. Worried that the etched ghoul's arrival will blindside her, she denies her eyes the right to blink, and the ventilation's arctic air that smells of day-old blood turns her tears into ice sculptures.

As the ghostly shadow figure infiltrates the white clock, the ticks grow louder, like giant footsteps stomping on a collection of brittle skeletons. Filling the entire timepiece, the spreading shadow seeps through a crack in the glass and lengthens onto the wall in front of her.

She immediately recognizes the manifesting figure as one that has been haunting her dreams for years and continually torments her with cognizance of deep-rooted disdain. Looking down at her disfigured hands, she is horrified to see that the portrait on her desk has been replaced with the creature's name.

"Shadow Monster," the invisible bodies around her chant with a thunderous tone that causes the clock's glass encasement to shatter.

Chloe has a front-row ticket to delving into hell, and she is terrified. The expanding dark shadow finishes its exit through the clock's broken glass and forms into the shape of a tall, stilt-like creature with a contorted face. Looking up to the decaying ceiling, the Shadow Monster's mouth juts open to a grin.

Squirming in her seat, she tries one last time to escape as the monster's long, skeletal fingers extend towards her desk. As Chloe's mobility has diminished to that of a stroke victim, she watches in slow motion as each of the Shadow Monster's needle-like fingers taps the desk in front of her. "Chloe, Chloe, Chloe!" the Shadow Monster snarls as the rest of its body joins its tapping fingers.

Stacking upon itself, the immense figure looks down at her. "Chloe, Chloe, Chloe," the Shadow Monster screeches like ungreased car brakes. Desperately avoiding eye contact with the ghoulish creature, she closes her eyes to minimize her fear and pretends it does not exist.

The Shadow Monster's pointed finger springs up from the desk like a switchblade and stabs through the cartilage of her chest wall. As the creature possesses her body, her face distorts like a twisting hurricane, and her enlarging eyes resemble a Kewpie doll.

She helplessly sits still as her pupils turn into black marbles that exit from her irises and roll across the floor. Hovering above the child, the Shadow Monster conducts the leftover whites of her eyes to roll back into her skull and provokes her body to seize convulsively. Her legs spasmodically kick while a sizable empty desk at the front of the classroom forcefully stops the rolling black marbles with ornate claw feet. "Chloe, Chloe," whispers a soft female voice.

The comforting nature of the voice's tonal quality pierces the isolation-stricken air.

"Chloe Chloe..." the voice whispers again in Chloe's ear.

This time, she hears the clarity of the voice heighten, and, at the peak of her demise, her troubled eyes leap open to see a concerned face. Hyperventilating from the horrible nightmare, it relieves her to see her teacher, Mrs. Shelly, wearing her typical modest clothing with a tight, slicked-back bun and heavy brown tortoise shell-rimmed glasses that reflect the overhead fluorescent lighting. She has a soft nature about her.

She touches her hand to the panicked child's desk. "It's all right, Chloe. I didn't mean to frighten you," Mrs. Shelly gently says.

Ignoring the kind words, Chloe frantically scans the room for the creature that had tormented her. Instead of finding the ghoul, she is met by the cruel faces of her laughing classmates. Curious about what has stemmed their chatter, she notices a stream of warm pee running down her leg.

Mortified, she quickly crosses her ankles to hide the accident.

"Hush, class!" Mrs. Shelly sternly says to the children. Racked with guilt for startling the child, she tries to diffuse the students' laughter. Chloe slumps and cowers further in her seat to hide.

"Sh! Everyone quiet!" Mrs. Shelly shouts louder to the unruly class.

To help with Chloe's embarrassment, she removes her blazer and wraps it around her lap. Sprinting to the front of the classroom, Mrs. Shelly points to a sign halfheartedly taped to the green chalkboard.

"Okay, class, repeat after me: kindness is contagious," Mrs. Shelly says as she clears her throat. The children redirect their attention to the chalkboard as they eagerly fidget in their seats.

"We are not mean, children; we are caring," Mrs. Shelly slowly states to the class. Watching each of the children's expressions, she makes eye contact with each face to make sure everyone is listening. Motioning with her hand, she signals Chloe to the front to join her.

Reluctantly standing to her feet, she walks to the chalkboard and hides behind Mrs. Shelly.

"Class, kindness is what?" Mrs. Shelly asks and waits for the energetic children to complete the latter half of the statement.

The kindergartners yell out a mess of random words to guess the answer. "Is CONTAGIOUS!" the class screams. The loud enthusiasm causes Chloe to shield her tomato-red face from further embarrassment.

"Excellent, children," the teacher states with warm satisfaction.

The sound of the bell ringing over the intercom incites the children to become restless. Mrs. Shelly waves her hand above her head to get the class's attention. "Now, remember, Monday is show and tell, so be sure to bring in your most favorite item that you would like to share with the class," she shouts with enthusiasm as the children grab their backpacks to leave.

Shaking her head and chuckling at the ridiculousness of the kids' ignoring nature, Mrs. Shelly turns her attention back to Chloe, who is huddled behind her. While kneeling to comfort her, she is interrupted by a small boy skipping to the front of the classroom wearing coke-bottle glasses and a half-tucked shirt.

"Mrs. Shelly?" asks Jake Mathews as he adjusts his stance so that his alligator rain boots avoid stepping on cracks. The small boy recently received a fresh haircut from his mother, and his hopping made the structure of his hair resemble a soup bowl bobbing in the wind.

"Yes, Jake?" Mrs. Shelly patiently asks.

Knowing that Jake Mathews craves attention, she anticipates a theatrical show, and putting on a fake smile; she turns her attention away from Chloe.

"Um... um..." stutters the boy as he clicks his heels together.

"Is everything okay?" the teacher asks with an inpatient sense of concern.

Even though he struggles with attention deficit, his behavior seemed more fidgety than usual. The teacher worried that she might be blamed for a second child wetting themselves if he needs to use the bathroom.

Spinning around in a spastic circle, he makes a grand gesture to his alligator boots and springs forward to land with his feet in the center of the next square tile. The alligator boots are dark blue, with ocean waves on the top and an alligator snout at the toes. "What if I already wore what I want to bring to show and tell?" he nervously mumbles.

Concerned that he may have missed his opportunity to make the rest of his classmates envious, he kicks his feet out in front of him like a marching soldier, making the alligators move. The commotion makes Chloe curious and clutching Mrs. Shelly; she peers around her legs to look at the dancing shoes.

Her intrigue turns to anxiety as she watches the alligator boots come to life. The reptile's spinning eyes suddenly protrude from the rubber, and the creature's sharp teeth project from the toes. Slowly, saliva drools from the mouths of the monsters, and their tongues hiss like a striking snake taunting her.

"Chloe..." the reptile whispers as its four legs sprout talons for nails. The friction from each of the toes creates a screeching sound as they scrape the floor.

Gasping with fear, Chloe plugs her ears, shielding herself from the sound.

Paying no attention to her uneasy nature, Jake continues to tap each boot like he is performing a tap dance.

"I love alligators! They have scales and teeth and swim," he states with excitement as he stands on one leg and pretends to swim through the air.

Chloe clutches her waist tighter, and Mrs. Shelly glances to see that she is okay. "I think that is amazingly wonderful, Jake, and I am sure the class will love to see them again on Monday," she says.

"Okay, good," he says with a sigh of relief. Proudly looking at his rubber boots, he continues to tap them with excitement as he moves towards the exit.

"Bye, Mrs. Shelly! Bye, Chloe!" he happily shouts with a wave.

Peering around Mrs. Shelly to look at his alligator shoes, Chloe notices they are back to normal.

"What do you say to Jake?" Mrs. Shelly softly asks her with a light nudge. Patiently waiting by the exit for a response, he bats his eyelashes.

"Bye, Jake," Chloe whispers under her breath.

"Goodbye, Jake, see you Monday," Mrs. Shelly says with excitement as Jake Mathews leaves.

Making sure that he is left the room, she removes her superficial smile and turns to Chloe. "Is everything okay, Chloe?" asks Mrs. Shelly with genuine concern.

"Yes, ma'am, everything is okay," Chloe softly says, avoiding eye contact.

Analyzing the child's shifting gaze, Mrs. Shelly notices the deep circles sitting like whirlpools underneath her small blue eyes. "Chloe," the teacher says. Moving closer to the anxious child, she continues to soften her demeanor.

"You know that if anything is wrong, you can talk to me. When I was your age, I had a mommy and daddy who were not nice to me," she casually states. "Are your mommy and daddy nice?" she asks quietly.

Afraid to answer her teacher honestly, Chloe restrains her words, triggering each vertebra of her spine to tighten and her jaw to clench. Sensing the tension, her teacher swiftly switches her approach.

"Let's get you cleaned up," says Mrs. Shelly as she lightly pats Chloe's shoulder.

Refusing to move, Chloe plants her feet to the floor like rooted tree trunks. "My mom's here," she whispers.

Looking at the exit, Mrs. Shelly spots Chloe's mother's pinched face and gaunt cheeks. The woman's stance accents the door frame like a weeping willow tree, and her messy, dirty blonde updo highlights her wasp-like features as she silently taps her foot.

Looking down at the pee mark on her dress, Chloe nervously shifts between standing positions to hide the stain.

"I thought I told you to meet me outside," She snarls as she crosses her arms. Flinching to avoid eye contact, Chloe fixates her attention on the leftover finger-paint stains on the floor.

Seeing the victim-like tendencies in the child's behavior confirms the teacher's suspicion of child abuse. She tries to intervene passively.

"Yes, mother. I'm sorry, mother," Chloe mutters.

Chloe's mother cracks each of her knuckles like a countdown for a bomb about to detonate as she attempts to mask her annoyance.

"It was my fault," Mrs. Shelly interjects. "I was just telling your daughter... how great she did in class today, and that it is all right to have messes sometimes," she says, stumbling for a storyline.

Pointing to the oversized blazer wrapped around the little girls' waist, Mrs. Shelly shifts her approach to empathize with the child. Seeing the off-colored blazer slumped around her daughter's hips brings a look of sheer disgust to her mother's face.

"Take that off, now!" she shouts as she snaps her fingers. The deathly scowl from the woman triggers a systemic reaction in Chloe, and her body trembles.

Trying to boost the mood, Mrs. Shelly runs across the room to the children's cubbies and snatches the run-down duffle bag that hangs from Chloe's designated hook. After making sure the bag is zipped with her belongings inside, Mrs. Shelly notices the rough exterior is covered with dark stains and worn holes.

"You know, I have spare backpacks if you would like one for her," Mrs. Shelly says as she reluctantly gives the adult-sized bag to the child.

Taking the duffle from her teacher, Chloe cowers at its appearance. Her mother impatiently motions for the child to come and points down at a spot on the floor next to her in the doorway. "Now!" her mother yells.

Humiliation falls over Chloe's face as she removes the blazer from her waist and timidly hands it back to Mrs. Shelly.

"I was just trying to help," Mrs. Shelly states.

Seeing that her daughter is not moving at a fast enough pace, her mother aggressively pushes past the teacher and grabs hold of Chloe's spindly arm. "Come on, Chloe! I said let's go!" she hisses with the aggression of a venomous snake.

The volatile nature of the situation forces Mrs. Shelly into a state of shock, as she cannot do anything to save the child from the emotional battery.

Chloe blindly follows her mother out of the classroom exit. Stunned in disbelief over the woman's volatility, the teacher flinches at the door slamming behind them.

Without an ounce of care, Chloe's mother continues to pull her child down the school hallway. Each turn that leads to a new corridor seems like a pitiless pathway to hell for the little girl.

The lackluster fluorescent lights above are almost burnt out, leaving their route deviously illuminated and causing the dimly lit walls to appear sinister.

Compelled by a deep urge to plant her feet, Chloe stumbles behind her mother. Hearing the faulty pitter-patter lagging behind her prompts her mother to pull harder as she laughs and grins at her victorious moment of squishing the passive teacher's self-esteem.

As her mother opens the final door to the outside world, Chloe shields her eyes from the flood of light.

Seeing that the school parking lot is almost empty reminds her mother of how late she was to pick up her child, and she laughs at the fact that she does not care.

A small line of cars waits patiently to greet the remaining children, guided by a woman named Sheila. The woman stands tall with pride and accomplishment. Encompassing a plastic whistle between her lips, she relishes the fact that she had recently been recognized as the number-one volunteer by the parent-teacher association, which provided her a reputation to uphold. Her pick-up coordinator uniform, a bright orange reflective vest, boldly adorns her favorite outfit, a long denim jumper layered with a chocolate-brown turtleneck.

Sheila invincibly stands next to a raucous group of young children who can barely contain their excitement for a weekend full of activities. Every student wears a yarn lanyard that loosely hangs around their neck to signal their parent picking them up or riding the bus home.

As Sheila flags the car in front of the line to leave, she ushers a new one into its place and scans the sea of children for the matching youngster. Spotting an apprehensive preschool girl with perfect pigtails, the woman releases the whistle from her pursed lips, allowing it to dangle by its bedazzled chain. Lowering herself to the ground, she calmly addresses the timid child, who is frightened by the line of cars. The little girl nervously tugs on the yarn necklace that hangs around her neck. Its picture of a tractor signals her designated pickup location.

Sheila smiles and points to a name tag stuck to her denim pocket. A sharpie-drawn smiley face dots the letter I in her name, and the child bashfully smirks. "My name is Sheila. You know, that is such a cool train," the PTA mom says with a warm grin.

Pointing to the tractor that hangs from the child's neck causes her lips to make the sounds of a running motor. The little girl wiggles with excitement at the compliment and giggles at the funny sounds.

"I'll tell you what, sweetie—since your Mom is here, I can hold your special necklace and keep it safe for next time," she softly states.

As she motions to the car, pulling up to the front of the line, she extends her hand. The small girl nods and passes her lanyard to Sheila for safekeeping.

The sound of the car's passenger-side window rolling down excites the child. An attractive young mom dressed in business attire and a Bluetooth earpiece leans across her seat to shout to her daughter. "Mommy missed you so much," the young mother says. Seeing her mother's face with sunglasses sparks the little girl to light up with excitement.

Hearing the loving exchange makes Chloe jealous, and she stiffens her legs to look.

"How was school?" the child's mother asks with an enormous smile. Thinking of how she would respond compels the girl's tiny body to jump up and down. "Fun!" she yells.

Sheila holds her hand as she skips towards the waiting vehicle, assisting her into the back seat as she waves at the mother.

The mom makes eye contact through her rear-view mirror. "I'm glad you had such a wonderful day, sweet pea," the girl's mom says. Leaning towards the passenger window, she waves to Sheila. "Thank you!" she shouts.

"Don't mention it," Sheila responds.

As she shuts the car door, a gigantic smile falls over her face. The greatest joy of her job is participating in every child's enthusiasm as they are reconnected with their parents.

Stuck in a daydream, Chloe fantasizes about the childhood she could have experienced with a different mother.

Irritated by her daughter's failure to move, she yanks Chloe's arm, and just as the car at the front of the line is about to move, she pulls her across the street.

"Stop! I didn't say you could walk yet!" Sheila frantically yells. Blowing her whistle, she sprints to save them.

The car's brakes release a loud screeching sound as the vehicle abruptly stops, and the shrill squeal sets Chloe's mother over the edge. Stopping dead in her tracks, she pivots to face the paused car angrily, then turns her rage toward Sheila.

"You don't even have a real job!" Chloe's mother yells in the middle of the sidewalk.

Offended by the words, Sheila proudly straightens her reflective orange vest and clears her throat. "My kids are my job. I'm a part of the Parent-Teacher Association," Sheila says with confidence sprinkled with purpose.

Before she can finish speaking, Chloe's Mother rolls her eyes and laughs.

"Kids are a job—what a fucking joke," she sarcastically shouts. Resuming her tight hold on her daughter's arm, she drags her towards an old red Suburban sitting on the outskirts of the parking lot. The sight of the car's smashed bumper makes Chloe cringe. Finished with their journey, it relieves her that her mother has finally let go of her sore limb.

Rummaging for her keys in a grocery bag she uses as a makeshift purse; her mother accidentally knocks an empty shot-size bottle of whiskey onto the asphalt and watches as it rolls. "Shit," her mother says under her breath. Lunging for the tiny plastic cylinder, she snatches it up from the ground. Still holding the small container, she allows her few free fingers to resume their search for the keys.

Finally finding them, she opens the car door and tosses the empty bottle onto the passenger seat floor. Chloe stares at her mother as she hops inside and starts the car, leaving her daughter in the cold. Rolling down the window, her mother's actions do not compare to the fantasy interaction she witnessed earlier. Instead, she begins to mock her ruthlessly. "Are you stupid?" her mother asks with laughter.

She hits the unlock button as she watches her daughter attempt to open the heavy back seat door. "If you don't hurry it up, I'm going to leave you here," she says with a sneer.

Sheila hears Chloe start to cry from across the parking lot and sprints to her to fulfill her PTA promise. She could not sleep at night knowing that she had not satisfied her duty of helping every child get home safely.

She sticks her head further out of the driver's-side window, continuing to yell at her struggling child. "It's not rocket science, sweetie," she states with sarcasm.

Reaching the chaotic scene, Sheila glares at Chloe's mother while helping the little girl open the door. The heroic nature of the PTA volunteer disgusts her, and she pretends to dry heave loudly. Not receiving the confrontational rebuttal she would like from Sheila causes her eyes to roll dramatically.

Grabbing Chloe's duffle bag, Sheila ignores her mother and boosts her into the car. Gently, she places the worn bag on the floor in front of her feet and lightly touches her knee. "There you go, sweetie," Sheila says with a smile.

Staring with desperate eyes, Chloe watches the PTA mom start to close the door beside her. With the door not fully shut, the smell of burnt rubber accompanies squealing tires as her mother peels out of the parking lot.

The harsh abruptness of the departure leaves Sheila in a cloud of confusion. "You're welcome?" she shouts.

Still staring at the car speeding away, she politely waves.

Chapter Two

THE GREEN DOOR

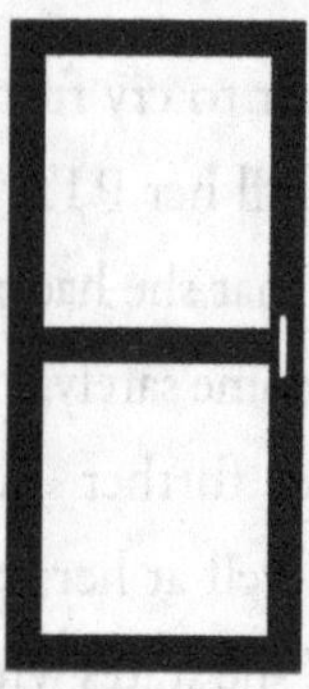

Unable to bear another moment of silent treatment from her mother, Chloe attempts to distract herself by staring out the backseat window. She is met with a consistent backdrop of depressed farmland highlighted by ghastly tinges of brown from an ongoing drought while watching the scenery roll by.

Despite refraining from looking in the direction of her mother sitting in the front seat, she can still feel the severity of her worsening glares in the rear-view mirror. Chloe is knocked away from her trailing thoughts by the fluttering sounds of the Suburban's failing exhaust, warning her she is nearing home. Mirroring the thickening tension, spattering smoke from the hood passes by her window.

The drifting smoke reminds her of each lit cigarette that her mother has puffed after completing enthralling punishments upon her. She gulps at the thought of what may ensue upon their arrival. Chloe trembles at the visualization of the hellish inferno that hides behind the house's front door and turns the whites of her mother's eyes a tinge of orange.

While passing the final acre of burnt crops, her eyes are greeted by a single crow sitting in the neighboring field. Hearing its loud squawk elicits her to feel empathy as she sits in the isolation of the backseat, yearning for any hint of companionship.

As the gravel road fast approaches, her mother lays her foot heavier against the red Suburban's gas pedal, and the ride becomes turbulent. Chloe's mother smirks as she delights in the car wheels peeling against each of the driveway's rocks.

Flinging gravel hits the sides of the beaten-down car as the flowing willow trees on either side create a tunnel, guiding its return. Clapping each side of the vehicle, the branches form a sound like applause for the duo's anticipated arrival. The car's increasing velocity creates gusts of wind that cause the passing trees to sway back, giving glimpses of an old, isolated 1920s-era southern manor. As she gets nearer to the estate, she can see the white paint that has been stained yellow by murky rain and the broken wooden porch with rotting floorboards and weeds grown between each crack.

She watches the window beside her, painted wet by the willow trees, leaving a smeared, dewy residue. Looking past a bending branch, she can see the sky's gloomy gray color as it prepares for a downpour of rain. The depressive tone makes her feel that something above is listening to the tears pent-up inside her tense body.

Raindrops begin to trickle from the sky, triggering the red Suburban's windshield wipers to wave. Each movement of the car's wipers reveals a clearer view of the overgrown yard surrounding the house's front porch.

The decrepit estate resembles an ornate plantation home with a sense of apocalyptic abandonment, and the sight of the cold exterior sends dancing shivers down her neck. The breathing of the young girl shallows as the chugging engine calms and the brakes screech to a painful stop.

Chloe's mother turns off the vehicle and aggressively pulls the keys from the ignition. Grabbing her purse from the passenger's seat, she catches her fingernail on the seat's cracked red leather, causing her face to flush with anger.

Terrified by her mother's seething rage, Chloe shoves her hands underneath herself to stay still, believing that if she refrains from movement, her mother may forget she exists in the backseat and leave her in the car.

Although the plan had seemed foolproof in her adolescent mind, she did not account for the seasonal pollen in the air, and, after wiggling her nose to stop an oncoming sniffling sensation, she releases a high-pitched sneeze. The sound drives her mother's tension to a whistling boiling point.

Glaring at her daughter in the rear-view mirror, her eyes turn a hateful shape as she stares into her panicking soul. "You are disgusting," Chloe's mother says with a sadistic chuckle.

Trying to behave like her mother's vile words do not bother her, Chloe pretends not to hear. She looks down at her muddied shoes to avoid eye contact.

"Just look at yourself!" Chloe's mother yells with a snarl. Wanting to ensure her daughter is listening, she abruptly slams the door to make a dramatic exit from the car.

Forced into a sudden moment of silence, she is left to her thoughts, haunted by her mother's volatile words. Looking at the yellow pee stain on her dress, she is embarrassed by her existence, and, fighting back her self-loathing tears, she closes her eyes.

Before she can catch her breath, the car door jars open beside her, and her mother grabs onto her forearm and plucks her from her seat. The movement's violence forces Chloe's seat belt to unbuckle, leaving lacerations across her stomach. Her frail body is effortlessly tossed to the ground.

Seeing that her daughter's bare knees are imprinted with small rocks from falling to the gravel floor causes her mother to laugh as she viciously throws her school bag for her daughter to catch.

"Don't be lazy. Get up," Chloe's mother shouts. She commands the child to rise to her feet using her snapping fingers. Chloe trembles as she stands up.

Continuing to mock the child, her mother shoves her in the direction of the rickety front porch and pushes her onto the rotted decking. Eager to see if the decayed wood supports her daughter's weight, she snickers at the sight of Chloe's dirty shoelace catching on a splintered piece of lumber. Instead of the usual calming orchestration of creaks, each step typically brings this time; watching her daughter risk her life brings only soundless disappointment.

Unentertained, she hurries past her child to the front door and smiles. Greeted by the entry's ornate brass knob, she knows that the object opens a portal to Hell and enthusiastically watches in hopes of seeing its steaming heat rise into the frost-filled air. The door hides her treacherous playground of hateful revenge, and that brings her a sick sense of joy.

The sight of her mother's finger's fondling the doorknob terrifies the child. Clutching the dirty duffel bag in her arms tighter, she tries to comfort her tiny, shivering body with the article's familiarity.

As her mother twists the handle, her lips spasm in a sadistic grin, causing her to slow down her pace. The metal under her grip instigates her masochistic satisfaction, and she wants to prolong the euphoric high.

Being aware of the house's haunting facade, she has little fear for passing looters and routinely leaves home without securing the lock. Flinging the door wide open, she closes her eyes to listen for the sound of the door crashing into the wall to welcome her. She takes a deep inhalation and tastes the stagnant air's pungent mold, and the odor's familiarity grounds her.

Opening her eyes, she twirls her body around to face her daughter, who is frozen in the cold. Pretending to feel pity for her child, she swiftly moves behind her to show sympathy. Reaching her hand over her daughter's shoulder, she offers to carry the tattered duffel bag.

As Chloe lifts the bag above her head for her mother to grasp, she remains blind to the cruel intentions unfolding behind her. Skimming the tips of her fingers across the backside of the canvas bag, her mother grins as she quickly retracts her hands.

Then, without taking a beat, she lifts the black patent heel on her right foot into the air and kicks the unsuspecting child's spine.

As Chloe falls beyond the threshold, she skids across the unfinished wood floor and revisits the pain from her gravel-scraped knees. She winces at the sound of her mother's footsteps entering the room as she continues to hold onto her duffel bag tightly.

Chloe buries her head in her wet bag, refusing to look directly at her mother. Her hearing heightens as she solely relies on her ears to warn her of the impending peril. The front door slamming shut sends vibrating shock waves through the dry-rotted walls, emulating an earthquake. As the rhythmic sound of echoing high-heeled footsteps approaches her, the cymbal-like beat of the clinking metal keys abruptly stops.

Wanting her daughter to pay attention to her entrance, Chloe's mother chucks the rusted set of keys at her head. Removing her small hand from the comfort of her duffel bag, Chloe clenches her throbbing skull.

"What did you tell her?" shouts Chloe's Mother.

Growing impatient with her daughter's lack of response, she begins to stamp her foot against the rotten wooden floor. Her tenacity creates a hole like a termite.

Unable to pull the child's attention away from her hurting head, she changes her body language. Approaching her daughter, she realizes the concussed aftermath caused by the flying keys, and her nose releases a swine-like snort. Coiling her fingers, she tightly wraps her hand around a musty strap of the duffel bag, and, using immense force, she yanks it from her daughter's single-handed grip.

As the bag is torn from her weak arms, Chloe pinches the air like a crab underwater, anxiously grabbing for the only sense of security she has left. Her mother loses enjoyment in the game and carelessly throws the duffel onto the floor next to the door.

A wave of anxiety floods Chloe's bones as she watches her mother's focus slowly return to her. Grabbing the dress's pee-stained skirt, she scrambles to cover the emotion on her face from her judgmental mother.

Just as her mother starts to focus on Chloe's new way of avoiding eye contact, she notices something in her peripheral vision. Overcome by a familiar worrying sensation in her gut, she observes her mother's fit of rage intersected by her shifting attention.

The large object that catches her gaze across the room is a curio cabinet with broken latches. Carved with roses along the perimeters, one of the doors appears to have been glued shut with tile caulking, and the other rests on a single malfunctioning hinge held together by a discolored rubber band.

Luring her mother, the rubber band snaps, and the falling door reveals an extensive collection of alcohol. Hearing the noise from the red-and-camel-hued door hitting the floor causes her posture to stiffen as she glides toward the siren call. Standing toe to toe with the diverse spread of liquor ushers an irreplaceable warmth into her core as she scans the shelves' contents. For a moment, the array of bottles prompts her to forget about her daughter. Suddenly her eyes lock on the sight of her favorite whiskey, and she drools. As she pulls the cherished bottle from the shelf, her eyes apologize to the other unchosen containers.

"Don't you worry, I will be back," the woman states to the remaining bottles of alcohol in a tone resembling a mother talking to an infant.

During her babble, she remembers that her daughter is lying on the floor behind her and clearing her throat; she uses the glass neck on the bottle to point in Chloe's direction. "You see what you make me do?" she shouts.

Chloe's mother manically chuckles as she begins to unscrew the cheap top off the bottle of whiskey. "You keep me from being sober," she says with anger.

With the last twist of her wrist, she removes the cap; wasting no time, she chucks it over her shoulder for good luck. Turning her attention back to the cabinet, she notices a large cup in the shape of a blue elephant with the trunk as the handle sitting on the second shelf. It reads My First Circus.

When initially buying the mug several years back, she had intended to preserve a memory that she wished never to forget, but now, the sight of the cup brings nothing more than a painful fit of rage that starts in her toes. As the emotion continues to work its way up her body, the pain turns her vision fuzzy.

Attempting to mask her self-hatred, she forces herself to snatch the cup by the elephant's trunk. Removing the mug from the shelf, she pours half of the remaining bottle of whiskey into it. Her eyes fill with deadness as she turns to face her daughter. "You are the reason I have to keep going back to fucking rehab," her mother's voice shudders.

Maintaining an eerie deadpan expression, she chokes down every drop of the cup's remnants. Locking her jaw to hide her horrific emotional pain, she shifts her attention to a standalone vintage record player that sits next to the cabinet. The record player sits on open shelving with mid-century walnut legs. It was the only well-maintained piece of furniture in the living room.

Before placing the whiskey bottle with its missing top under her arm, a drop of leftover residue falls from her lips, and using her palm; she wipes it away. "You want me to die, don't you?" Chloe's mother shouts over her shoulder. Shaking on the floor behind her, Chloe covers her ears to ignore her words.

Her mother crouches to get a better look at the collection of records. The contents within the stack of albums appear to be primarily new, except one that strangely sits alone. Unlike the others, it is without a sleeve, and the face looks worn with scratches.

Holding the chosen vinyl in the light to get a better look, she traces her finger along each new scratch she finds. Each war wound brings a vivid memory to her mind and a genuine smirk to her face. After blowing away the sitting dust from the record's grooves, she places the vinyl on the player's platter and watches as the music turns on. Anticipating the sound of the needle hitting the vinyl's surface, she patiently waits for permission to start.

Taking another gulp of whiskey from the bottle, she hears her anticipated cue and turns her body to face Chloe. The stereo speakers amplify a melody of ghostly familiarity that makes Chloe squirm. She has listened to the song before, and it typically has not been associated with good memories.

Her mother makes her way closer to her and lets out a loud chuckle. "You want me to drown in alcohol, don't you?" she shouts sarcastically.

Her mother's fast approach triggers Chloe to hug her knees and curl into a ball tightly. As she gets down on the floor, her mother reluctantly uses a part of her daughter's soiled dress to cushion her soft knees from the splintered planks. Lowering herself down further, she begins to hiss in her ear. "I bet you want a fucking drink," her mother softly says.

Watching her daughter's terrified eyes refuse to acknowledge her presence annoys her. Waving the cartoonish elephant cup in front of her child's face, she tries to get her to look into its eyes. "Does that make you happy?" She screams in a condescendingly mocking tone. Unable to control her anger, she chucks the empty cup across the room.

Chloe shakes her head no in hopes of diminishing her mother's mounting fury. Rather than defusing the situation, the lack of verbal response only causes her mother's escalating intoxicated mind to further fixate on her daughter.

She trembles upon feeling her mother's grip take hold near the vicinity of the dark yellow stain. "You think I enjoy treating you like this?" She asks while laughing sarcastically.

Waiting for her daughter's lack of rebuttal makes her seethe with anger. "Answer me, you little cunt!" Chloe's mother yells in Chloe's ear. With her handful of stained material, she spirals and slams her fist with the dress against the wooded floorboards.

Chloe flinches as she tries to muster the courage to articulate a complete sentence. She shakes her head. "No, ma'am," she mutters timidly. As the words fall from her distressed lips, tears trickle like the first rainfall down her flushed cheeks.

The notion of witnessing the monster of fear engulf her daughter's sanity fills her mother with a deep sense of accomplishment. While pondering ideas to enhance the moment's fun, she raises the open bottle of whiskey to her lips and takes another sip. "Why don't you try some and see how it feels? Maybe then you wouldn't be such a horrible child," Chloe's mother says with a smirk.

Moving the open bottle of alcohol above Chloe's head, she starts to laugh at the sight of her daughter's hands attempting to shield her mouth. Torturing her daughter, she drips the burning substance over her eyes to get her hands to move from her lips. "Why don't you see what you put me through? Come on, open your mouth!" Chloe's mother yells and spits with anger.

Leaning over her child, she forces her daughter's hands away from her face. She squeezes her daughter's cheeks between the fingers of a single hand, and the pinched puckering forces her mouth to open. "Remember, no one likes a brat," her mother says in a vindictive tone.

Beginning to pour the whiskey into Chloe's mouth, she watches as the liquid pools to the brim of her teeth and overflows down her chin. She is not alarmed by the sounds of choking that ooze from her child's throat; instead, she becomes jealous of her daughter drowning in alcohol. Stopping her hand mid-pour, she takes a swig.

"Since I know you think I treat you so horribly, I'm sure you are just dying to go live with Sheila from the PTA," Chloe's mother says with a snarky tone.

Chloe's cringing face makes her mother feel sadistically gratified as she watches the last bit of alcohol enter her burning esophagus. Carried away by the punishment, she takes a moment to bask in the glory of her daughter's small whimpering sounds.

Her demeanor abruptly shifts as she grows concerned that if she pushes her frail body any further, her plans for future manipulation may be ruined. Watching her daughter use her hands to mask her face, she erratically softens her facial expressions to match the emotion of her child.

"If you think you have it bad, you should have seen my childhood. It was Hell," she reluctantly says. Thinking of her treacherous childhood memories, she pushes herself away from Chloe.

Even after being treated like day-old trash, Chloe still sympathizes with the woman. Hearing the pain in her mother's voice brings about a sense of guilt, and she peers through her fingers to check on her emotional state.

Her daughter's attention gives her a sick sense of satisfaction, and she internalizes it as if it is a call for a mental encore, inciting a grand finale of her theatrical performance.

Mimicking her daughter's huddled position, Chloe's mother pretends to shudder with fear. "Trust me, if you had pulled that shit on my mother—oh, boy, you would have been sorry," her mother says. Continuing with her introspection, she crawls with her whiskey bottle closer to Chloe and playfully taps the tip of her nose.

"One thing that is for sure: no one would be able to recognize that cute little face ever again, "Chloe's mother states matter-of-factly. Pitying the thought of not being the one to cause damage to her daughter, she shakes her head with disappointment.

Shock falls over Chloe, and her skin turns stark white. Her mother watches a single teardrop fall from her eye, and pretending to comfort her, she wipes it away.

"Hush, baby. Momma's here," she says.

With her daughter's head falling into her lap, she immediately knows that she has successfully trapped her in a cycle of manipulation. She quickly finishes the last drop of whiskey left in the bottle and sets it on the floor to caress her daughter's head. "You remember when I walked into your classroom to pick you up today?" She softly asks.

Chloe responds with a timid nod confirming her compliance. Assured that success is within her reach, her mother moves ahead with her interrogatory agenda. "Now tell your sweet momma what the nice teacher said," her mother warmly whispers.

A train of sniffles builds from Chloe's small nose as she gathers her breath to speak. "She asked—she asked if I was okay," she quietly stutters. The words passively leap from Chloe's trusting lips as she nuzzles her head deeper in her mother's lap.

Shoving her daughter off her thighs, she is angered by the fact that the child's vague words did not match her preconceived storyline. "Ungrateful!" she yells with rage.

While searching for her words to say, she springs to her feet to pace the length of the room. "You're ungrateful just like that other little shit—just like your brother," she says with hateful energy.

Trying to intimidate her child, she towers over her to belittle her. "Piss stain and all," she says with a cackle.

Noticing her mother's condescending tone when mentioning her younger brother stirs mixed emotions inside Chloe. Putting on a brave face, she clears her throat to speak. "Where is Timothy?" Chloe asks.

To deflect the question, her mother grabs the bottle from the floor and gulps air from the container, forgetting it is empty. After realizing the container is void of liquid, she tosses it aside. "Who?" she casually asks.

"Timothy," she states, after clearing her throat to speak louder and with more confidence.

Hearing the name makes her mother deeply uncomfortable and causes a look of disgust to imprint on her smug face. "Oh, him," Chloe's mother says with a shrug.

Attempting to brush off the emotional flurry that Timothy's name internally triggers, she fixates her attention on a green door that sits underneath the large staircase by the entryway. The delightful image of the splintered door brings a grin onto her stern lips.

Seeing the emotional shift on her mother's face makes Chloe curious, and she looks for the source that fuels her newfound happiness.

"If you think I'm so bad, just wait until your father hears about your day at school and all of your little piss-filled shenanigans," her mother says with a chuckle. Taking her daughter's face between her hands, she redirects her attention to the stairs, and Chloe's body stiffens with terror.

Chloe is horrified by the sight. Fighting away her tears, she frantically pleads for forgiveness and bends over her mother's heels to grovel.

"Please—I didn't mean it. I swear I will do anything you ask," Chloe says, floundering for mercy. Looking up to her mother's eyes, she watches as every bit of compassion leaves. "Please, mommy, please don't make me go down there!" she cries.

She notices her mother showing no signs of empathy, and she crawls backward to escape. Lunging forward, she grabs Chloe's tiny limb. The emotion her trembling body exudes adds an overwhelming sensation of invincibility to the woman, and her confidence grows.

"You can wait for your father in time-out, reflecting on every terrible thing that you have done in your short existence. If you are lucky, you may even run into someone you know," her mother states.

Mustering up all the energy she has left, Chloe tries to pull away from her mother's brutal grasp with all her might. "Please, I'm scared, momma. Please don't make me go down there. There's a monster that will eat me!" Chloe screams, pleading for her life.

The thought of a monster eating her child brings peace to her mother's mind.

"Guess you should have thought about that before you decided to embarrass me," her mother states coldly, shrugging.

Desperation sweeps over Chloe's body as she fights to survive. "Momma, I didn't say anything, and I didn't mean to have an accident. I swear I didn't. Please, momma, please," Chloe cries.

Ignoring her daughter's building cries, her mother remains entranced by the dark green door and the harmony that it selfishly promises her.

"Please don't make me go down there!" Chloe shrieks as she grabs onto her mother's legs.

Reaching down to her daughter's stooping head, Chloe's mother interlaces her fingers through a knot in her tangled hair. She smiles from ear to ear as she drags her across the floor.

As she tries to stop her mother, the sounds of screams leaving Chloe's dry throat mask the sounds of her kicking feet. "The monster is going to get me!" Chloe shrieks in terror.

Watching the green door getting closer, she plants her feet against the floorboards and tries to slow her momentum. "It's going to get me!" she screams at the top of her lungs; her mother is annoyed by the high-pitched shrills.

Suddenly, the motion stops, and her mother's grip eases, signaling to Chloe that they have reached the gateway to the fated plunging staircase. The ominous door sends shock waves down her spine and paralyzes her muscles.

A thick green welding apron hanging on a rusted nail next to the door complements the door's out-of-place color scheme. Releasing her daughter's hair, she grabs the rubber apron off the nail and fastens it behind her neck.

"I promise, I will be good, momma. I love you. Please don't do this. I'm scared." Chloe says.

Continuing with her usual routine, her mother ties the apron around the back of her waist and pulls an ornate skeleton key from the pocket. The clicking sound of the tarnished key unlocking the basement door extinguishes Chloe's thoughts of hope.

"Monsters don't exist," her mother says with forceful laughter.

Sadistically finding pleasure in her daughters' terror, she watches her facial expressions as she slowly opens the entrance in front of her. Low whispers echo from the darkness at the bottom of the basement staircase. "Chloe, Chloe, come join us," whispers a near-inaudible deep voice that mimics a low, howling wind.

The nondescript echoes sound like music to her mother's ears. Closing her eyes, she tries to match the tone by amusingly humming along. Suddenly, her eyes reopen. She grimaces at the sight of the terror manifesting in Chloe's pupils and gives her back a nudge. "Go on, girl. Get in," her mother playfully commands.

Shoving her daughter inside the dark abyss, she slams the door shut behind her.

Chloe tries to escape from her nightmare by tightly closing her eyes. Reluctantly reopening them to look, she discovers that she is still surrounded by the same darkness and gulps as a loud echo stems from the sound of the door locking behind her.

As she awaits the inevitable, the anxiety of the unknown causes prickling pain to radiate down her spine.

She is trapped.

Chapter Three

THE BASEMENT MONSTER

Lack of light in the basement has rendered everywhere she looks pitch black. The room's darkness creates an unwanted veil over Chloe's face, and her features become unrecognizable as she blindly feels for the stair railing.

Silence suffocates her sensitive eardrums. Every unexpected creaking sound sends panic running amok through her mind. Her thoughts spiral off the sound of each foreign noise as her lucid nightmares continue to play gruesome tricks. The heaviness of her breathing ramps up louder to match her heightened anxiety. She intently listens for any noise that could signal she is not alone, and the piercing scratch of the record player needle switching songs on the other side of the door stops her search.

"Your father will be home within the hour, and he can deal with you then," she yells from the living room. Even though her voice is muffled through the sealed door, Chloe still shivers from the inflection. After her mother is done speaking, her ears are met with silence.

She jumps at the sound of a new song starting to play from the living room. Listening closely, she shivers at the tune's familiarity. Each note plays a soothing melody with an eerie timbre she associates with her father, and the dark realization makes her tremble.

Looking back to the locked door behind her, she reluctantly accepts that the only direction she has left to escape will lead her to the bottom of the basement stairs. Timidly picking up where she left off, she searches blindly for the stair railing and is relieved when her trembling fingers seize hold of the worn, waxed wood. She slowly guides her feet down the rotting staircase one step at a time.

"This doesn't exist. This isn't real," she murmurs. Taking shallow breaths, she tries to convince herself that she is dreaming. "It's all my imagination, just like the song," she says.

As she tries to calm her racing heart, her feet come to a stop. Using the toe of her worn shoe, she taps for the next step in the darkness and is shocked to find that her foot is met with the unforgiving resistance of concrete rather than the usual flex of wood. The realization that she has safely reached the last step of the stairs relieves her.

Continuing to feel the solidarity of the basement floor under the tip of her foot brings a false sense of security to her young mind, and she becomes careless. As she makes a leaping descent off the last step, the wood releases a loud creak. The echoing sound shocks her and fills her with regret.

Reaching the solid ground, she hears something scurry in the distance. Assuming the sound is from a monster, she crouches on the cold, damp floor and helplessly waits for the beast to permanently end her mental exhaustion.

"He... hello?" a small boy's voice stutters in the distance.

The recognizable stutter of the boy's speech immediately kicks Chloe out of her depressive state. Focusing all her energy on the direction of the timid voice, she makes out the outline of curly hair in the distance. Squinting through the darkness to get a closer look at the child wearing a stained white shirt, she connects the voice to her younger brother.

"Timothy?" she quietly asks. Unable to contain her excitement, she jumps to her feet and runs to hug him. Embracing her brother, she can smell that he has not showered in days. Taking a step back, she notices his more-disheveled-than-usual appearance and becomes concerned. Wanting to ask him what happened, she starts to take a breath and opens her mouth to form a sentence.

Seeing his sister begin to purse her lips to speak causes him to panic, and he holds a single finger up to his mouth. "Shh!" he whispers.

Like clockwork, Chloe hears heavy footsteps echo behind them. Looking at her brother, she watches as the whites of his eyes get bigger with fear. "It's going to hear you," he quietly states with a lisp.

His eyes nervously dart in the noise's direction and pause. The sound of the giant footsteps filling the air drives Chloe to match his reaction and freeze.

"It-it's here," Timothy states with a stutter.

The stressed tone behind her little brother's words immediately tells Chloe that the creature joining them is the very thing she has been dreading most. Knowing she must look, she releases Timothy's shoulders from her trembling hands. Slowly turning to face the direction of the noise, her teeth begin to chatter together with terror. Her erratically darting eyes confirm her nightmarish suspicion as she sees the outline of a tall, bony frame standing tilted in the distance.

The approaching entity is the Basement Monster.

The vile creature has gaping black holes for eyes that can turn any child's soul into stone. Its rotted jaw is blotted with worn jester makeup that has oxidized, causing every pore to divot like a dried sponge as each layer of the caked-on toxic paint stains its decaying skin. Spindly limbs that look like twigs come from the monsters' sides. Dark clothes resembling an oversized work suit hang effortlessly from its emaciated form with a large dark burgundy stain embedded in the aged fabric. Atop its head is a dusty bowler hat that is slightly too snug for its swollen skull, and the creature's feet wear heavy work boots stained by bloody gore.

The physical vividness of the monster sends utter panic through Chloe's chest, worsening her shaking knees. She cannot look away.

A loud cracking noise ruptures the dead air as the Basement Monster stretches his neck from side to side. Refocusing on its surroundings, the creature extends a single leg to take a slinky step forward.

Still in shock, Chloe turns to face her brother. "Hide," she whispers with panic.

Blindly motioning behind her with her jittery hand, she signals for him to get on the floor and take cover. Timothy holds his breath as he lowers himself to the ground and crawls under a welding table.

Hearing the children scurrying in terror sparks the creature to whistle a happy tune. Walking to the song's beat from above, the monster's heavy footsteps mock the children's terror.

Timothy, afraid to release a single exhalation, remains quiet in his hiding spot as he watches his sister hide across the room in the bottom of an antique wardrobe.

Continuing to hold his breath in fear of discovery causes the small boy's lungs to begin wheezing. Gasping for air, he begins to panic.

The sound of heavy footsteps abruptly stops.

Chloe hears the commotion and peers from her hiding spot to look. Realizing that her brother's anxiety has triggered an asthma attack, she feels as if the scene is unfolding in slow motion in front of her.

Still whistling a merry tune, the Basement Monster slowly lowers himself to the cold concrete to look for the heavily breathing child.

"It's only make-believe," the monster sings with a high-pitched giggle. Spotting the child under the welding table triggers the creature's broken jaw to form a half-toothed grin.

Unable to breathe, Timothy cannot scream. Desperately grasping for oxygen, he spirals into a frantic state of shock.

As the clownish terror leans forward to get a closer look at the little boy, a red circular nose topples from its soiled front shirt pocket. Tilting its head down, the creature patiently watches the red ball bounce in the boy's direction. Then, contorting its limbs, it extends a pointed finger with a long-cracked nail toward the crimson snout. Blindly stabbing the air, the creature tries to harpoon the sponge-like material, grunting as the claw-like digit continues to miss its target.

As it wildly gouges the space surrounding the little boy's hiding spot, the erratic movements cause the nose to roll closer to Timothy and stop next to his shaking foot.

Adjusting to the ball's new position, the monster's head slinks in unison with its reaching appendage to better search under the welding table.

Timothy desperately clutches his throat for help. The only thing on his mind is trying to disappear from the horrific scene. Coming to terms with his morbid fate, he closes his eyes to visually numb himself from the anticipated pain of the creature's devouring teeth.

The monster creeps closer to the frightened boy with shuttered eyes and peeps with a single eye socket to get a better look, then slinks to the back of the table. "Gotcha!" the monster shouts.

The sight of the nose next to the child's enticing foot makes it salivate. Extending its tongue towards the scarlet proboscis, it stretches until contacting the prized possession, then licks it up. The object travels down its esophagus, releasing a dying squeak as he swallows it whole. The noise makes the creature laugh hysterically as it regurgitates until the sphere pops through a crater of cartilage on its face.

Saliva accumulated from the laughter projects onto Timothy's cheek, and he closes his eyes tighter.

Amused by the child's attempt to disappear, the creature wishes to reciprocate the magic show by performing a trick back. Giggling to get the boy's attention, it licks its contorted face as it uses its elongated hands to cover its empty eye holes.

"Peekaboo, I see you," the Basement Monster states with building excitement. Hearing the familiar words that start his favorite game entices Timothy to open his eyes to look.

Peeking through its fingers, the creature checks to see if the child is watching. Seeing the rotted face peer through its pointy appendages terrifies Timothy. He struggles to scream for help as his asthma attack escalates. Frantically he searches his pockets for his inhaler.

The evil entity blatantly ignores the severity of the situation and playfully mimes with its fingers. As if putting on a puppet show, it pretends its spindly digits are walking legs traveling towards the small boy's quivering foot. "How's my favorite little boy?" the creature asks with a snicker.

The words cue a fighting response in Chloe that forces her out of her state of shock. Watching her brother frozen helpless as his face turns blue prompts a rush of adrenaline to race through her veins. Quickly scanning the floor, she spots his inhaler lying in the area where their earlier reunion had taken place.

Crawling from her hiding place, she hears the wardrobe door loudly creak. The Basement Monster's head shifts directions to look.

She immediately freezes and glances towards the welding table, inadvertently making eye contact with the creature's glare. "Someone's looking just like their mother," the monster says with a flirtatious giggle.

Knowing that she is the only hope for her brother to survive, she tries to ignore the monster and crawls faster.

The creature slinks out from under the welding table and licks its lips as each limb stretches like a fucked-up spider towards Chloe. "Irresistible!" The Basement Monster says while releasing a shrill scream of excitement.

Realizing that the creature is entirely out from under the table, Chloe knows she only has seconds to grab the inhaler. Climbing to her feet, she sprints to the device and kicks it in her brother's direction.

Timothy's body is on the verge of collapse as the inhaler slides across the concrete floor. Wriggling in the device's direction, he hurries to get the medicine to his mouth.

The sight of Chloe's bare leg poking out from under her dress as she kicks the inhaler makes the Basement Monster leave a trail of drool that glistens on the floor.

"You look so delicious. I could eat you up," the creature squeals with its snaking tongue.

Chloe shifts her gaze away from the monster to check on Timothy. Seeing her brother puffing his inhaler boosts her will to survive.

Positioned in front of the girl, the creature takes its time to unravel its elongated body from its crouching position. The sight of its carcass-covered bones stacking upon one another mirrors the erection of a skyscraper. Each rising layer creates another element of terror reflected in the pupils of Chloe's widening eyes.

As the monstrosities excitement heightens, its entire body begins to vibrate. Its frame shakes violently that the red clown nose peels from its face. Hanging by a tiny sliver of putrefied skin, the red ball sways with the creature's jarring momentum.

Still frozen with paralyzing fear, the spectacle makes her stand in a petrified tremble.

Using two of its fragmented bone fingers, it plucks the nose away from the rotted piece of flesh and begins to juggle with it. "Want to see a trick?" the Basement Monster asks.

Chloe hesitates to answer as it squeaks the rubber ball in its hand, then apprehensively shakes her head yes.

The lackluster response from the child disappoints the creature. Rotating its head upside down, the monster lets gravity force a lopsided frown across its malfunctioning jaw. "You're making me sad," the monster cries.

Black tears fall onto the floor from its twisted face as if from cartoonish sprinklers. The creature intently stares at the boy and commences its performance, juggling the dingy clown nose on its terms, regardless of the children's engagement.

As it does, Chloe contemplates her next move, surveying the surrounding contents of the basement.

The clown-like fiend becomes complacent with the ball's whereabouts in its juggling act upon being distracted by the dangling flesh that had once held the orb to its face falling like a unique black-and-green snowflake. The juggling ball misses its hand as it sticks out its tongue to catch the skin.

The red clown's nose gathers dust as it quietly rolls towards Chloe's feet. Not realizing the nose is gone, the monster rotates its head in circles to signify the show's grand finale. "You want to make me sad?" the creature asks with a pout.

Its tone mimics a person's voice after consuming too much helium, and the high pitch hurts Chloe's ears. Taking a step backward, she covers her ears to soften the sound. "No... no, sir. No, Mr. Basement Monster, sir," she whimpers as she stumbles for what to call the creature.

The monstrous name that she bestows on the gruesome being irritates its ego. It pauses its performance to glare daggers at the girl. "I'm not a monster!" the creature shrieks with a vicious snarl.

Scared by the shouting, she trembles as she thinks of another name. "No, Mr. Clown Man," she states cautiously.

Afraid of his response to the new title, she slowly tiptoes backward to getaway. Fixated on his growing reaction, she becomes unmindful about the placement of her steps, and the clown's nose squeaks under her foot, causing her to jump.

The Basement Monster hears the noise, looks down at its juggling hands, and realizes his nose has disappeared, "You just made my day, little girl!" the monster says.

Amused by the challenge, it tries to place its spindly thumb between its two fingers. "I just love games!" the monster shrieks.

Moving its bony digits closer to its face to get a better look, it treats the stuck thumb like a jigsaw puzzle. "Don't you love games?" the Basement Monster says with a manic laugh.

Trying to mask its annoyance from the thumb not cooperating, the creature aggressively breaks it into place and triumphantly grins.

Unlike the monster's jubilant reaction, the sound of the shattering tactile member causes the young girl to wince.

The clown dances with glee. "I got your nose," It shouts, giggling with pride as it shows off the finger formation it worked hard to create.

Seeing the fractured bone jutting from its large knuckle terrifies Chloe. She frantically pats her face to check if her nose has disappeared and turns panic-stricken when the tip of her finger slips into an indented hole. Only peeled-up skin rests where her nose used to be and tickles her metatarsals.

Coming to terms with the fact that her nose is gone sends a waterfall of screams from her throat.

Entertained by the child's panic, the creature laughs with a sound comparable to an off-pitch organ playing church hymns.

"Give it back.... give it back!" she cries uncontrollably.

Stuck in a horror-filled frenzy, she watches as the Basement Monster dances its hands around one another. Bringing them to an abrupt stop, the creature reveals a tiny child's nose is sitting between the same three fingers and fractured thumb. "This one?" the Basement Monster asks.

Chloe looks with horror as she continues to cover the gaping hole in the middle of her face with her shuddering hands.

Using its opposite hand, the creature reaches behind its emaciated torso. Pulling its closed fist from behind its back to show the girl, a look of surprise falls over its lopsided grin.

"Or..." the Basement Monster says. Tapping its bloody work boots against the concrete, the monster creates a makeshift drumroll with its feet. Building the percussion to a grand crescendo, it opens its fist and reveals a plethora of small, severed children's noses.

Chloe gasps.

"...one of these?" It says with delight.

Using the crater on its face, the creature smells each of the prizes it has collected. The evil entity smiles, exposing its sharpened teeth, pleased by the stench of iron that wafts from the collection of tiny appendages.

The little girl shrieks.

Ignoring her fear-driven squawk, the creature continues to admire each of the noses proudly. Taking a moment's pause, the monster mentally recounts every story of how each was found—or, more often, stolen.

"Took quite some time to get this collection," the Basement Monster says.

Refusing to close her bloodshot eyes, an alarming amount of anxiety forces all Chloe's joints to stiffen.

Observing her trepidation makes the creature smile. "If you can guess which one is yours, you can have it back," the Basement Monster declares.

Watching the child turn a shade of green, the creature flings its hands through the air like a glider plane. Showing all the options for her to pick from, the fiend ramps up its enthusiasm. "Which one is it?" It announces like a carny operating a center joint at a carnival.

Masticating upon Chloe's hesitating decision, the Basement Monster quickly pops three of the noses into its mouth and chews them loudly, each bite generating its mouth to open wider. The sound of crunching cartilage echoes through the darkroom. Timothy covers his ears and nose as he hides in the farthest corner underneath the welding table.

As the creature finishes swallowing the carnage, it opens its mouth to show that everything has been devoured.

"Stop, Mister! Please stop!" Chloe wails.

The sound of the child begging invigorates the vile being. One by one, it stabs its jagged nails through each remaining nose and howls with laughter as it puts on a puppet show by wiggling the noses impaled on its claws.

"This little piggy went to market," the Basement Monster says in a frenzy of animated excitement.

Allowing the first little piggy on its pointer finger to take a final bow, it tosses the nose into its mouth. Licking the delicious taste from its lips, it uses the heavenly flavor as ammunition to continue.

Boosting its next finger higher than the rest, it begins to wiggle the next nose. "This little piggy went home," it says in a somber tone filled with cynicism.

Before the sadness can manifest into a frown, the monster quickly chucks the second nose into the back of its dark esophagus to swallow. Getting rid of the gloomy pig makes the clown maniacally happy.

Cheerfully wiggling its next finger, the creature uses its tongue to caress each drop of its dripping saliva. "This little piggy ate roast beef," the Basement Monster sings with a cheerful spirit. Popping the nose into its mouth, the taste from the skin's salty pores spawns its body to jiggle jubilantly.

Pausing for a moment, the monster anticipates the next piggy's sad story and becomes irritated. The creature reluctantly forces its finger to move, not wanting to perform the fourth part of the children's rhyme. "This little piggy had none," it says in a monotone voice. Feeding off the pouting tone, it swallows the nose with no enjoyment.

The traumatic scene causes Chloe to melt to the ground, hiding her face between her knees.

Seeing that she has been knocked into a permanent state of shock brings the creature irreplaceable joy. Smiling at her misery, the Basement Monster holds the final severed nose out for her to behold. Its large, jagged nail pierces through the center of the small nostrils and leaves the flesh barely attached to the septum. The notion of seeing what the disfigured nose may look like reattached to the child's face excites the creature.

"And what did this little piggy say?" the Basement Monster asks with a loud giggle. Waving the skewered nose through the air, the creature playfully tiptoes towards Chloe. Hovering over the child, it waits for her anticipated reply.

"Stop! Please stop!" She shouts.

Not appreciating her response, the monster allows her one last chance for redemption. The child listens to the creature's tapping foot next to her.

"Make it STOP!" She screams.

Chloe sobs hysterically as she watches the Basement Monster grow disappointed by her answers lack of creativity.

Switching the direction of its performance, the monster begins a portion of improv. "We both know that's not how the piggy story goes," it states in a miffed tone.

Crouching to the floor, it leans its upper body closer to the child. Refusing to look, Chloe buries her head deeper into her lap.

"Wee, wee, wee, wee, all the way home!" the Basement Monster shouts in her ear.

Unnerved by the proximity of the voice, her eyes jerk open, and she finds herself face-to-face with her mutilated nose teetering from the creature's long nail. Her mouth gapes wide to bellow for help, but her vocal cords cease to exist.

"What's the matter? Cat got your tongue?" it asks with a cackle. It opens its mouth unnaturally wide to suck in air like a vacuum. The panicked child watches as the creature inhales the clown's nose from the floor and swallows it.

Sticking out its tongue to show that the nose has vanished prompts the nose to pop back through the crater on its face like a weasel surprising a hunter from a dirt hole. "Now it's your turn!" it says.

Leaning closer, it lightly brushes her disfigured nose against her refusing lips. Moving its finger around her bobbing head, the creature pretends to be a train as it tries to find another opening.

"Here comes the Choo Choo," the Basement Monster yells as it demonically slithers its finger to ram the freshly severed nose between her pursed lips.

Timothy watches the terror build in his sister's eyes from his hiding spot underneath the welding table. Knowing that he is too small to fight the entity makes him feel helpless. Looking at the inhaler in his hand, he is reminded of how she has saved his life, and he knows he is the only hope of doing the same for her.

He sees a white light switch outline near the basement stairs in the distance. Acting impulsively, he begins to crawl towards it.

Still fighting for her life, Chloe senses a dripping bloody mixture of mucus from the septum's tattered skin painting her lips. Closing her eyes, she tries to escape from her feelings of nausea.

The monster senses her fright. Sticking out its tongue, it tries to pry her lips open to feed her the nose. "Open wide, baby girl. Don't make me force it," it screams.

The lights abruptly flicker on, followed by the needle on the record player scratching to an abrupt halt.

Chloe's eyes jolt open as she sees the color under her eyelids shift to a brighter tone. Slowing down her breath, she can see that the Basement Monster has strangely disappeared. She frantically pats her face for her missing nose, and finding her nostrils brings her confirmation that she is safe.

She looks toward the welding table and notices her brother is missing. Desperately scanning the room, she spots startled Timothy with his hand holding the light switch. Chloe immediately runs and hugs him to thank him for saving her life.

"Come on, Timothy. We have to hurry before it comes back," she says.

She trembles as her eyes dart around the basement to check their surroundings. Not seeing any monsters, she tightly grabs onto her brother's hand, and they bolt up the basement stairs. Stopping at the top step, Chloe looks directly into Timothy's eyes.

"You remember what I told you?" Chloe asks.

Timothy looks to the ground and nervously searches for what words to say. "You're my big sister?" he quietly guesses.

Chloe takes hold of her brother's shoulders and pulls him closer to listen. "No matter what comes our way, we do it together," she says.

A loud creak sounds from the basement door in front of them. Slowly looking up in fearful unison, they see that the exit has mysteriously cracked open.

"We have each other. It's okay as long as we have each other," Chloe says, in a reassuring manner to comfort her brother and convince herself.

The basement lights flicker behind them, then shut off without warning. Both children look in panic at the door in the pitch-black darkness.

Tugging on Chloe's dress, Timothy fixates his gaze on the warm light coming through the unlatched passage in front of them. "You promise?" he asks.

Chloe glances to the bottom of the dark basement and hugs Timothy. "Promise. Cross my heart and hope to die," she states confidently.

Inhaling a deep breath, she signals for Timothy to join her. Taking his hand, she places it under hers on the door in front of them. At that moment, she knows that their emotional strength will get them through the darkest of times and lead them to safety if they have each other. That alone provided her a feeling of irreplaceable comfort.

Chapter Four

THE LIVING ROOM MONSTER

The children hesitate before exiting the basement. Peering through the doors cracked opening into the living room, they notice something peculiar. The area looks a bit more cynical, now accented with darker tones. Every window blind is pulled shut to block out the outside world, and with no light entering the room, a dull film is cast over the curio cabinet's bright colors. Two white candles glow in the room's corner near the lightless windows. A warm flickering glow from the candles' flames contradicts the horrible trauma the children have faced. The home's dungeon-like ambiance evokes cold shivers to drip like leaking faucets down their frozen spines.

Chloe takes a deep breath as she nudges the basement door open a fraction more. Tentative to be brave, she bides time by nervously clearing her throat and tightening her grip on top of her brother's hand to gather emotional support.

Leaning her head out from behind the basement door, she looks for any sign of life. Monster or not, she is terrified of hearing any response that would signify the children are not alone. "Momma?" she quietly calls out to the bleak space. Listening for a reply, she releases a sigh of relief that there is no answer.

Timothy encouragingly taps her hip to try again. "Are you there?" she asks a little louder. Wanting to make her brother happy, she uses a more chipper tone to pretend like she wants to see her mother.

Met again with silence from the living room, a sense of serenity fills her adolescent mind. Closing her eyes, she promptly gives thanks to the heavens for delivering them to a safe space. In the middle of her sincere gratitude, she hears faint whispers sound from the bottom of the basement. The chain of deep echoes forms chilling waves of vibrations through the children's ears. "Chloe... Chloe... Chloe..." the voice piercingly whispers. Each word grows louder, sending the siblings into a mental frenzy.

Neither one wishes to relive the last occurrence, so they dart through the exit in unison without further hesitation. Breaking into a dead sprint through the living room, the children run toward the front door to escape.

Halfway across the darkened room, Timothy abruptly plants his feet against a softened wood floorboard and parks himself on the ground. "What if Mom needs us?" he asks with a pitiful whimper. Though he has been mistreated in the past, the thought of being orphaned is overwhelming, and panic over further abandonment sets in.

Trying to get her brother to stand up, Chloe tightens her grip around his hand to pull him forward. "She's fine. She's an adult," she says.

Upset by the thought of leaving his mother and refusing to budge, mournful whines sound from the little boy's core like a puppy after losing its toy.

In disbelief that her brother wants to help the woman who continues to neglect them, Chloe rolls her eyes. "Come on, Timothy. I don't know how much time we have," she says, pulling on his hand with a sense of urgency.

Throwing a tantrum, Timothy's frizzy brown curls bounce as he shakes his head. "We have to go now!" she shouts. Squeezing his hand tighter, but his body is stubborn and refuses to move.

Escalating into an emotional meltdown, he anxiously tugs back on her hand as he boorishly kicks his feet in a fit of an outburst. "I want mom!" he screams. Using every ounce of his oxygen to call for his mother turns his face a shade of bright red.

Not wanting him to create a scene that attracts unwanted attention, she reaches down and grabs his shoulders to defuse the situation, and with all her force, she spins him around to face the green door that betrayed them. "Timothy, look— she doesn't care about us," she exclaims.

Seeing that her brother still refuses to listen, she tilts his head to look in the door's direction. "She let the monster have us!" Chloe states. She hopes the visual combined with her harsh words will get her brother to listen.

The memory associated with the sight of the putrid green door makes Timothy squirm uncomfortably.

"We don't need her. We have each other," Chloe says.

Timothy's deep-seated torment stemming from his time in the basement swirls inside his mind and triggers his body to fidget nervously. Scooting to face his sister, his eyes begin to well up with tears. He can scarcely process his recent horrific experience involving the monster and let alone his suppression of any past trauma.

"Wha... what... what if the monster gets her?" Timothy asks with a stutter.

Looking down at her brother, she catches a glimpse of her soiled dress, and a flood of painful memories infiltrates her mind. Remembering the appalling way her mother treated her earlier in the day makes her brother's lack of mutual disdain for their mother even more frustrating. She considers his desire to save her over them validates her mother's abusive words about her worth.

"What if it does?" she asks. Seeing that her words bother Timothy makes her happy. By upsetting her brother, she believes she has attained passive revenge on her mother due to her blatant favor of him. "She doesn't care about us," she says.

Refusing to listen to his sister's unsympathetic words, Timothy desperately tugs his hand in an attempt to release her grip. "Yes, she does, Chloe," Timothy sobs.

The emotional cry of her brother makes her dramatically roll her eyes. Feeling her suppressed anger build, she tightens her grip around her brother's tiny hand. Timothy winces from the pain. "No, she doesn't, Timothy!" Chloe shouts.

Stubbornly refusing to listen to his sister, he pulls his hands away and uses his fingers to plug his ears.

"Did you not hear anything I just said?" she asks. Signaling her frustration, she throws her hands up into the air.

Switching her method to get her brother to side with her, she grabs her face to reenact the terror from the basement. Tremors run through her hands as they cup her nose. "The clown man almost ate my nose!" she shrieks.

Watching her emotional improv, Timothy stubbornly burrows his ears in his tiny hands.

Using all the strength left in her exhausted body, Chloe tries again to pull her pouting brother to his feet. This time, her momentum works, and she gets him to stand. "I can't leave you here, Timothy," Chloe says with a grunt.

Continuing to tug him across the room, she ignores the silent treatment her brother is giving her. "The monster will get you!" she exclaims, trying to inspire his feet to move. But her attempt at sparking fear within her brother falls flat; he is unfazed by her dramatic words.

The sight of the nearby ornate doorknob brings haste to her tired limbs, giving her the motivation that she needs. She manages to thrust his limp body the rest of the way to the front door.

The doorknob's cold metal underneath her fingers forms an abnormal smile across her quivering cheeks. Not ever allowed to experience joy, the muscles in her face that would typically evoke a smile have never fully developed. What may seem like an act of second nature to many resembles a marathon to her.

Twisting the doorknob that will aid in their escape, she senses the smile accumulated across her cheeks ripped from her face. The locked door ruins all aspirations for happiness. Placing a second hand on the doorknob, she aggressively tries to pull the heavy exit open. Her brother stands still as he observes the desperation in her movements.

"Come on, let us out!" Chloe yells angrily.

As the stagnant door refuses to listen, an icy prickling sensation rolls into the living room like unwanted morning fog. Sensing a shift in the room's temperature, Chloe looks at her brother. Her eyes grow wide as she watches his exhaling breath imprint on the room's icy air.

Knowing that neither one had touched the turntable behind them, she jumps at the sound of the needle scratching against the vinyl, and it elicits a sinking feeling that something has been eyeing them during their attempted escape.

A foreboding clarity arises from the needle's scrape, and a song that carries a strange familiarity begins to play. Inhaling a large gulp of air through her shaking lungs, she reluctantly pivots to see who has started the music.

"Hello?" Chloe asks.

She is convinced she may see a figure; she squints her eyes at the distant darkness and timidly tries to get a better look. Still unsure of what she is calling to, she hesitates before trying again to get its attention. "Who's there?" she asks a little louder.

As her eyes adjust to the darkness, she can see the outline of a human frame.

A naked creature with a thin build stands next to the turntable.

It is the Living Room Monster.

The sinewy figure with long blonde hair faces the corner of the wall to hide her face from the children. Repetitively whispering in a derivative dialect of Latin, the thing recites old hymn lyrics with an iridescent melody.

Blood from its scalp trickles onto the unfinished wooden floorboards as it pulls out clumps of hair and throws them onto the planking. Picking up a grouping of single hairs from the floor, it takes each end between its fingers. Using the strands like a wire clay cutter, the Living Room Monster begins to saw at the inside corners of its mouth. Its tiny black marble-like eyes fixate on the blank wall as it finishes carving a permanent grin that connects each high cheekbone to the other.

Timothy becomes excited, convinced that he recognizes the figure masked by the dimly lit room. He aggressively rubs his eyes to improve the accuracy of his vision as he squints harder. "Mom?" he shouts excitedly.

Still deciphering the thing's identity, Chloe is afraid he may attract unwanted attention and tries to quiet him.

Sniffing the air with its bird-like nose, the sound of the small boy's voice catches the creature's attention. Snapping its head to look in their direction, its neck cracks as it over-rotates its skull. The loud noise sounds like a twig breaking and adds an unwanted snare drum to the music, frightening Timothy.

Following the loud clamor, its head topples to the side as it dangles by a single vertebra. Using its fingers to tilt its mangled head towards the ceiling, the monster allows each nostril to inhale a waft of the small boy's scent. The luxurious smell incites the flaps of mutilated skin on the creature's face to form a sinister smile. Three rows of needle-like teeth are revealed as the cut corners of its lips part. Each tip of the pointed yellow teeth is stained burgundy red.

"Hello, darling," the Living Room Monster whispers.

Unable to recognize the voice, the children's bodies become frozen. "No... no... no," Chloe whimpers. As she hears the mysterious voice, her imagination paints vivid portraits of what the being could look like. The scary thoughts stirring in her overwhelmed mind compel her body to shudder.

Not wishing to confirm their accuracy, she pounds her fists against the front door. "Help!" she shouts.

Receiving no help from the outside world, she slowly turns to look at the shadowed silhouette behind her. Becoming more terrified by the figure's emerging appearance, she frantically motions for her brother to join her in pounding on the heavy wood. Timothy ignores her pleas, his eyes remain fixated on the creature's stature, and he is convinced the entity could be his missing mother.

"Someone, please help us!" she screams at the top of her lungs. The vibration caused by Chloe's cry makes the Living Room Monster's grin broaden.

"Please!" she wails.

As the monster props its dangling head against the wall to look at the children, it licks the splits in its lips. It repositions its backward body to match the direction of its glaring marble eyes. "Such a pity to see a pretty child so upset," the Living Room Monster says with a demonic cackle.

Lifting its hands in the air, the creature hits the wall like a game of patty cake. Clicking its serpent-like tongue against its back row of teeth, it tries to grab the children's attention. "You can't want to leave already. We haven't even gotten to play any games yet," the creature says.

Chloe's fists begin to bleed as she pounds harder on the door. Failing to win the attention of the girl, the monster frowns. "So sad that no one can hear you, my sweet child," it says.

Running its long nails down the drywall, the creature pretends to play a string instrument to the beat of the music. "It's just you and me now, baby girl. That means only I can hear your screams, and only I can decide your fate," the

Living Room Monster says with a chuckle. She extends a vascular hand with thin purple skin and lures Timothy forward like a snake charmer enticing a cobra.

Tugging on his sister's dress, Timothy tries to get her to look at what is happening in the living room.

"Don't be afraid, children," it states.

Confident that he can trust the creature, Timothy strives to get his sister's attention by pulling on her dress with more force. "Chloe, maybe she can help us!" he whimpers. As he pleads for his sister to listen, he tugs harder.

Provoked by her brother's annoying persistence, she reluctantly turns to look at the scene unfolding behind her. Realizing that the monster's manipulation is working on her little brother throws her into a state of panic. She frantically places her hands over his eyes to cover them.

"You can't look at her, you hear me?!" Chloe anxiously shrieks. Prying at her gripping hands, he continues to try to get a better look at the mysterious creature.

"That's not mom, Timothy. That thing over there is just trying to trick us, like the other one from the basement," she says, trying to explain quickly.

Unhappy that her words may interfere with the manipulative hold over Timothy, the creature's face suddenly scowls. Squawking as if trying to summon open the gates of hell, it releases its bitter feelings towards the girl through high-pitched shrills that sound like scratching nails on a chalkboard.

Chloe covers her ears and focuses her attention back on escaping.

Instead of the unbearable noise heard by his sister, Timothy hears a voice that calls him like a siren. Seeing that his sister is no longer paying attention, he leans closer to look.

Slowly opening its mouth, the Living Room Monster reveals a thick blue tongue coiled in a ball like a sleeping snake. Noticing the little boy's fascination prompts the creature to unroll the decaying flesh fully. A shiny black marble sits on the end of the extended appendage. Every angle of the polished glass glistens in the nearby candle's flickering flame.

With its mouth still open, the Living Room Monster regurgitates a second black marble from the back of its throat. As its esophagus launches the shiny ball, it collides with the stagnant one like a game of pinball, and the momentum causes the first glass ball to fall to the floor.

Timothy attentively watches as the marble rolls across the wooden planks towards him.

The monster knows the child keeps a metal box filled with a collection of marbles under his bed. When choosing an object to attract him, it knew he would not be able to resist the glass ball's temptation.

Letting his yearning desire take over, Timothy runs to the marble and picks up the sparkling sphere to admire it. Filled to the brim with an overwhelming sense of joy, he twirls in a circle before showing Chloe what he found.

"Look, Chloe—so pretty!" Timothy says looking at the marble with fascination.

Irritated by her brother's unwillingness to help, Chloe ignores his childish ways and continues fidgeting with the door. "Stop it!" she yells over her shoulder.

Remaining focused on surviving, a series of tremors run through her limbs as she desperately shakes the doorknob harder. "We don't have time for games right now, Timothy. I have to get us out of here," she says.

Shrugging off his sister's unreceptive demeanor, Timothy shoves his new marble into his dirty pocket.

The Living Room Monster chuckles at the entertainment. Closing its sullied lips, the creature ejects the second marble across the floor towards Timothy's feet. The marble rapidly rolls, stopping abruptly in front of the boy's toes, and his legs twitch with excitement. Turning to make sure the troublesome door still occupies his sister's attention, he lunges at the stagnant marble.

Bending down to the floor, he admires every shiny speck that the marble projects on the ground like a disco ball, and each brings a new level of excitement to Timothy. "You can be friends with the other one," he says with a giggle.

While placing the marble next to the other in his pocket, he spots a glistening object out of the corner of his eye, sitting on the ground next to the record player.

"Ahhh," he says, gawking as his attention shifts to the mysterious item sitting across the room.

Acting like a peeping tom, the creature sits in salivating silence to watch.

Biting his lip with hesitation, Timothy thinks of the repercussions that may arise from his sister seeing him fetch the shiny object. Checking one last time to see that his sister is still busy picking the locked door, he makes a run for the sitting marble. The little boy grabs the glass sphere from the floor and causes a coy smirk to paint across his face. "You are my favorite," he says admiringly. Thinking of each fun game he can play with this brand-new addition brings him joy.

Carefully, he uses his delicate hands to place his most prized marble in his pocket.

Slowly looking up, he decides that he wants to hunt for more. Glimpsing another sparkly piece of glass just out of arm's reach, he extends a hand to try to touch it. He falls forward as he moves his feet closer. Watching the marble playfully jolt back into the shadows, he laughs. Timothy crawls towards the darkness to chase the glass ball and notices the pleasant sensation in his stomach flip to fright.

As he clutches his abdomen, he focuses his gaze and sees that the marble sits on the Living Room Monster's open palm. Overcome by desire, he reaches for the shining glass.

Enjoying the game of cat and mouse, the creature closes its hand. "Don't you want to help me, Tim Tim?" the monster asks.

Continuing to beg, the creature makes its voice more soothing. "You know I want to help you," it whispers.

Opening its palm, the Living Room Monster exposes the marble and watches the little boy squirm with excitement. "See, I'm not scary. Would you like another marble, Timothy?" the creature says with a friendly grin.

Taking one last look, he checks to make sure Chloe is not watching, then nervously moves closer on his quivering knees.

The Living Room Monsters' mouth opens more expansive, and a beautiful tsunami of marbles disperses across the wooden floor. Diving to the ground, Timothy frantically scoops up as many marbles as his tiny hands will allow.

Each facial laceration worsens as the monster's cheeks form an elongated grin, causing its head to lose balance.

Noticing that the marbles still mesmerize the child, the creature lets its head continue to dangle as it points a jagged nail in the child's direction. Its finger extends toward him, sprouting like a growing vine.

"I know where your mom is," it says with a snicker.

Hearing it mention his mother incites Timothy to gasp with excitement. He smiles as he looks up at the entity. "Really? You do?" he asks enthusiastically.

Across the room, Chloe continues searching for an alternate escape route and remains unaware of her brother's whereabouts.

The Living Room Monster's yellowed nail drifts inside Timothy's ear, causing him to giggle. "Hey, that's not nice! That tickles," Timothy says with uncontrollable laughter.

Lodging its nail further into the child's ear, the creature drags him closer. "I can show you where my innocent child. All you have to do is trust me," the Living Room Monster says with a demonic grin.

Dragging the child across the wood, it releases the jaws of its gaping mouth. As the orifice opens wider on its dangling head, its eyes roll back to prepare for the child's arrival. As he is pulled in the monster's direction, the terrifying sight makes Timothy scream.

The flickering candle lights burn out without warning, and Chloe is left alone in the pitch-black room. Shocked by the complete darkness, sparks paranoia to set in. Removing her hands from the door, she takes a moment to listen.

The sound of the creature scurrying onto the ceiling prompts Chloe to jump. Spreading her arms, she blindly traces her surroundings and notices that her brother is missing. "Timothy?" Chloe whimpers.

Her hands become frenzied as her search turns more frantic. "Timothy?" she shouts.

She blindly flails her limbs in the lightless space patting the air around her for her brother. Moving deeper into the room as she searches, she senses an odd tickling sensation sweep across her forehead. Assuming that an annoying bug is harassing her, she uses her hands to swat at the aggravating nuisance. Then, noticing that her swatting is not helping relieve the problem, she clutches what she believes to be the culprit.

"Gotcha, little girl," the Living Room Monster says.

Realizing that the object in her hand is a clump of the creature's stringy, long blonde hair triggers her entire body to tremble uncontrollably. She slowly shifts her eye line to view the ceiling overhead. Realizing that what lies in her grasp belongs to the monster above, she Releases her grip and screams with horror.

As the Monster slinks through the blackness, each strand of hair takes the form of a serpent that wraps tightly around Chloe's fragile neck. The constricting sensation around her throat makes her choke, and she gasps for air.

Effortlessly lifting the small child off her feet, it pulls her closer. Kicking at the air underneath her to gain any footing causes Chloe's shoes to fall off and land with light thuds on the floor.

The creature's mouth opens widely like an anaconda engulfing its prey as it lets out a rattling hiss. Salivating from the smell of the approaching little girl, the creature slurps up her hair like homemade spaghetti.

As she feels herself losing her last ounce of hope, Chloe hears a faint, muffled voice in the distance. "Chloe, help me!

I'm scared!" Timothy cries from upstairs.

Straining her bulging eyes, she tries to look at the staircase leading to his voice. Hearing the voice brings her a glimmer of hope that her brother is still alive, returning her will to endure.

Taking the last swallow of Chloe's hair, the creature sucks on the top of her head.

"Timothy, I'm coming," Chloe says, straining the words through her constricted windpipe.

The monster maneuvers her head towards its cavernous mouth as it continues to try to eat her alive. As the Living Room Monster begins to tighten its half-torn lips around Chloe's skull, it scurries back down from the ceiling.

Feeling the hair serpents slightly loosen from her throat, she tightens her eyes and lets out a blood-curdling scream.

The creature crouches deeper into the floor to inhale her panic.

Desperate to escape the horror, she closes her eyes as tightly as her lids will allow, shielding her view from the nightmare. As the torn mouth of the creature moves over her nose, she exhales one last scream for help.

The high-pitched tone of the shriek creates sound waves that shatter a bottle in the alcohol cabinet, and a shard of glass hits the spinning vinyl on the record player and forces the song to slow to a stop. Along with the silence, the living room lights flicker on.

Sensing the light penetrate her tightly shut lids causes a conversion. Immediately, she feels her head to see if she is dead, then opens her eyes and looks up to see that the creature is gone.

Glancing across the room, she sees her duffel bag still sitting on the floor from earlier. She runs and grabs it on her way to the door to escape. Realizing that the exit is unlocked, she is reassured, knowing she will soon be safe.

As she twists the knob, she notices a small object near her toe. Looking closer, she recognizes that the thing is a multicolored glass marble. She bends over and picks it up. Analyzing the intricacy of the swirling glass, she is reminded of her brother's marble collection and the games they would play together. "Timothy," Chloe whispers.

Still clutching the colorful sphere tightly in her hand, she looks towards the staircase. "I can't leave you, Timothy," Chloe says with confidence.

Slowly opening her hand, she analyzes the marble in her palm. "We have each other's back, no matter what... No matter what," Chloe says.

Focusing her attention back on the top of the stairs, she notices a flickering light and squeezes the marble for companionship.

"You can't be afraid. You've got to do this for Timothy. He needs you," Chloe states.

Motionless yet shaking with fear, she forces her feet to walk towards the staircase. The living room lights begin to surge as her foot reaches the first step. Worried that the Living Room Monster may return, she sprints up the stairs with duffle and marble in hand.

Chapter Five

THE PINK PAJAMAS

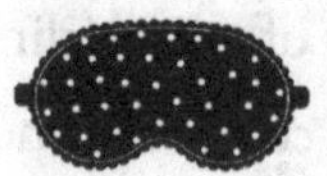

Chloe ascends halfway up the flight of steps, stopping to stare in the direction of the flickering light. She realizes it is shining from under her brother's bedroom door with a clear view of where the illumination is coming from. Distracted by the mesmerizing glow, she feels an odd sense of security, knowing that her brother could be safe in his cozy bed.

Taking a moment to appreciate the warm luminosity, her eyes follow each bouncing ray to see where they choose to land, and her glance is guided towards a progression of family photos that line the staircase wall. As she analyzes the images, she experiences deep-seated feelings of nostalgia.

Taking notice of the dancing light beams, she observes that a single hanging picture appears favored over the rest. Wanting to better look at the well-lit photo that sits dead center in the lineup, she shifts closer to the wall.

Stopping an arm's length away, she notices that it hangs crooked on its nail, unlike the other family photos. She carefully leans forward and nudges the portrait's dark wood frame to re-center it. After straightening it to match the rest, she begins to laugh at the scene encapsulated in the glass.

She notices that a layer of dust blankets the photo's encasement; she lifts her tiny hand to clean the portrait. Uncovering the filth from the left corner of the photograph, she recognizes a younger Timothy. He looks to be just shy of one year old. Seeing his little body clothed in a pair of cute yellow pinstriped overalls makes her smile. His face exudes utter happiness as he flails his tiny arms playfully in a pile of crinkled leaves.

Excited to uncover the remaining scenery, Chloe clutches her dress like a polishing rag and cleans the rest of the dingy glass, then analyzes the following individual in the picture through the frame's clear facing.

Recognizing the small girl sitting next to her brother, dressed in color-coordinated outfits, and playing in a pile of leaves brings her joy. Her two-year-old self is wearing a pastel-yellow bow on the top of her head that adorns a perfectly curled ponytail. The lower half of her dress is decorated with a vivid applique of bears having a formal tea party, and each bear seems more delighted than the next.

Reminiscing over the image of happier times, she cannot help but smile at the fun they used to have. At first glance, she does not recognize the woman sitting next to her in the photo, but she realizes that the cheerful individual is her mother after analyzing the image further. A genuine smile gleams across her face as her father kisses her cheek. The thought of her mother and father kissing makes her blush, and she giggles naively. "Eww, cooties," she says with a giggle.

Covering her eyes, she attempts to look away to shield herself from embarrassment. Peeling her fingers from her face, she places a fingertip on the portrait and carefully outlines everyone's silhouette, attempting to soak up the positive memory. She closes her eyes to make a wish, and before finishing her trail of thinking, she is pulled into the scene.

Engulfed by the intricacy of the surrounding ambiance, she believes that her wish has been granted. She thinks the details are much too believable to be a daydream. The rundown southern manor stands perfectly painted, back to its original pristine condition, and the wooden porch is freshly stained, with the needed repairs completed. A large willow tree sits in the front yard and sheds an abundance of yellowing leaves that fall into picture-perfect piles underneath.

Grabbing a textbook fall-colored leaf, Timothy places it in his toothless mouth. Watching her brother's googling eyes trying to concentrate on eating the foliage makes Chloe laugh. Their mother sits next to them, straightening up her lace apron and admiring her children with her porcelain-like face. She had purposely selected her modest Easter dress, with pastel-yellow-tinted lace, to coordinate perfectly with the clothing worn by the children.

She is thrilled at the opportunity to relive a single moment of happiness and ignores the uneasiness caused by the memory's eerily perfect demeanor. The cute family reunion mimics a page from a 1950s homemaker catalog similar to one her mother would idolize.

"You two are as cute as buttons," their mother states. Leaning towards the children, she wiggles her fingers and laughs. "Here comes the tickle monster!" She says with a playful voice. As she pretends to sneak up on her children, she watches them dodge out of the way to avoid her.

Trying to hide in the leaves, Chloe cannot help but giggle.

Pretending that she cannot see her daughter under her invisibility cloak of foliage, her mother reaches over her to tickle Timothy. As his face turns red from giggling, she gently taps his nose, and the baby's gurgling smile produces bubbles that sparks everyone to laugh.

Continuing to play with her children, she steps towards her daughter. "Tickle, tickle, tickle," her mother playfully says. Clearing the leaves from her daughter's hidden face, she kisses her forehead. Chloe's smile lingers from the tickling kiss.

The hinges from the front door loudly creak, causing the playing trio to turn and look towards the house as Chloe's father aggressively opens the door with a gleeful smile. The house's wall stops the momentum of the door with a crash. Dressed in a suit and work boots, his grin attempts to mask his tired demeanor from his strenuous day of labor. Springing into action, her father is over-animated as he waves to the children with his camera case around his neck.

"Whoa, there!" he shouts. Making his way down the porch steps, he chuckles at his springing pace. "Wait for me. I don't want to miss any of the fun!" he yells.

He matches his exuberant tone with his skipping feet. Watching their father's excitement build, the children become impatient, waiting for his arrival. "Daddy!" Chloe says excitedly.

While bashfully waving at him, she watches her daughter throw a pile of leaves like confetti to celebrate their father's arrival. "There's my handsome man!" she says.

Patting the leaves lying next to her skirt, she motions for her husband to join them. "Don't worry, I've saved the best seat in the house just for you," she proudly declares.

He happily accepts his wife's invitation and picks up his pace to a jog. Reaching the trio, he joins in on the fun, scooping up a handful of leaves, throwing them into the air, and watching as they rain down on the children.

The sprinkling of leaves causes Timothy to smile with his gums and stick out his tongue like a lizard. Thinking that his son's behavior is funny, Chloe's father fumbles to switch on the camera. "Why does he always have to do that when I least expect it?" he states.

As he hears the camera slowly turn on, he releases a sigh of defeat.

"I keep missing little Timothy making that adorable face," he says.

Still waiting for the camera to boot, he impatiently taps the side of the device as he aligns his eye to the peephole to line up the shot. The camera flashes without provocation, and it startles him. "I've got to get better about using this thing," Chloe's dad says.

Trying to keep his composure, he puts on a smile and pretends like the camera flash is a typical startup occurrence. Acting fast, he snaps another picture of the baby, then hits the playback button to check the quality. Excited about the moment he captured, he points at the camera's screen and forces his wife to look. "I mean, moments like these don't last forever," he says with a half-joking nudge.

Awkwardly joining with her husband's laughter, she shrugs off the depressing idea that her children may eventually want to leave her. "In a scrapbook, they do," she states with a smirk.

Wanting to match the playful tone of his wife, Chloe's dad gallops away like a trotting horse. Spinning around to look at his family, he snaps another shot.

She is miffed because she was not ready for the photo and repositioned herself to a flattering angle for the next. Content with her appearance, she motions for her husband to rejoin the family and sit next to her in the leaves.

"I'm trying to take some pictures for our invisible scrapbook. You know someday you will have to make one," he says with a sarcastic tone. She attempts to ignore her husband's underhanded comment but cannot help but react by dramatically rolling her eyes to show her disapproval.

Realizing that he has upset his wife, he immediately uses flirtation to cover his condescending tone. "What now?" he asks softly.

Noticing the shift in her husband's voice causes a sheepish grin to form across her face.

"You know, it's not technically a family photo if you are not in it," she says.

Confident that he is escaped the doghouse, he quickly turns on the camera's self-timer and sets the device down on a nearby stump. He runs to join his family in the pile of leaves and positions himself next to his spouse.

"Is everyone ready?" he asks.

Trying to catch his breath from the run, he jumps into position and scoots closer to his wife. "OK, everyone, say cheese!" he yells. Instead of saying cheese when hearing the third tick of the camera, he surprises his wife with a kiss on her cheek.

"CHEESE!" Chloe shouts.

The camera flashes, taking the photo.

Looking at her husband, she touches the damp spot on her cheek and blushes. "You sly fox!" she says with a hint of embarrassment.

She attempts to regain her composure by springing to her feet. Looking down at her dress, she notices that leaves have stuck to her skirt and frantically brushes them off. "Silly me!" she states with an awkward giggle.

To distract everyone from her frazzled state, she clears her throat. "I can be such a ditz sometimes," she mutters. Her husband tries lightening the mood by nodding in agreement.

"After spending half the morning preparing our food for the picnic, I can't believe I left the basket inside," she sheepishly states. Hearing her husband's taunting laughter makes her erupt. Angrily scowling at him, she waits for him to be silent before sprinting toward the house.

Eagerly watching his wife leave, Chloe's dad looks over his shoulder to make sure she has reached her destination. The door closing behind her prompts him to redirect his attention to the children. Turning back to face them, he halfheartedly laughs. "Want to play a game?" he whispers to Chloe.

Anxiously waiting for his daughter to respond, he looks back at the home's front entry to ensure that the coast is still clear. Her father's anxious behavior makes Chloe feel uncomfortable.

"Come on, don't give me that look, Chloe—it will be fun!" he says. Reaching forward, he pinches her nose.

Watching his daughter fling her hands to her face to feel for her nose makes him chuckle. He makes a fist with his thumb between his two fingers. "I got your nose!" he roars with a cackle.

Chloe's eyes grow large with horror as he shakes his fist in front of her. Nervously giggling, she masks her fear as her eyes go cross-eyed to look for her missing appendage.

Delighted by the display of his child's distressed behavior, he taps the tip of her nose like a magic trick. "See, it's back!" he says, cheering with excitement.

He glances again towards the house and smiles at the view of the closed door. Returning his attention to his daughter, he leans closer. "I'm not going to hurt you," he whispers.

Still suspicious of his demeanor, she scans her surroundings for ways to escape and reluctantly forces a smile onto her face to mask her fear. Sensing his daughter's timid nature, Chloe's dad moves beside her. "Calm down," he says.

She takes a deep breath and looks at her baby brother, distracted by the colorful leaves. "Want me to tell you a secret?" her dad asks in a high-pitched tone.

Her father's proximity makes her hesitant to answer, but after a moment's pause, she reluctantly nods.

Reaching into his back pocket, he pulls out a clown nose and watches her expression slowly shift as he secures it to his face. He slowly lifts his fingers to the red nose and gives it two squeaks. His daughter's squirming body puts a devious smile on his face. "Wake up, Chloe," he whispers.

As his words trail off into the breeze, the sharp cackles of the Basement Monster jolt her awake, and her opening eyes transport her from one dark scene to another. Tremors roll down her spine, and her body shakes as she realizes she is standing on the staircase.

Chloe excessively rubs her eyelids, hoping to rid her mind of both nightmares, and finds it disheartening that she cannot decipher which of the two realities is more horrible to live in.

Staring at the photo, which she thought to be a positive childhood memory, now seems like a deceitful lie. Stepping closer to the family portrait induces her skin to turn a shade of ghostly white. The scenery in the photo has shifted.

Now, in the picture, her father wears a clown nose while kissing her mother's cheek. Gasping with shock, she notices blood on her father's hands. An open wound surrounded by torn bloody skin in an oval-shaped pattern fills the place where her nose used to sit. Turning her attention away from herself, she realizes that her brother lays dead in the pile of leaves. Two shiny black marbles in place of his irises have joined his eyes.

Trying to process the details of the gruesome scene, she burrows her face into the crease of her arm to hide. "It's not real. It's not real," she mutters under her breath.

Sensing her eyes welling up with tears, she convinces herself that everything is okay and musters up enough courage to peek through her trembling fingers. Noticing that the photo has returned to its original state, her shoulders shudder with relief.

Scanning her surroundings, she takes a moment to process that she is safe, then fixates her gaze back to the top of the stairs. Determined to move forward, she views each *creak* of the rickety staircase as a reminder that she must find her brother.

Her foot placement on the top step causes her body to become stationary. Slowly adjusting her vision to the pitch-black hallway, she shifts her eye line to acclimate. "Timothy?" she cautiously calls to the darkness. She feels blindly around her body until her hand meets the closest wall. Standing motionless, she listens for a response.

"I'm in here!" a tiny voice shouts from a distance.

Hearing the muffled answer sparks Chloe to light up with enthusiasm. Confident that the voice belongs to her brother, she quickly readjusts her trajectory to follow the sound. "Stay where you are, Timothy. I'm on my way!" she says at the volume of a loud whisper.

Desperate to find him, she uses the lath and plaster to guide her travels down the dark hallway. "Don't move, Timothy!" she says.

Stopped by the wall at the end of the hall, she listens for the voice to guide her way. "Hurry, Chloe!" Timothy calls.

Turning her body in the voice's direction, she finds herself face to face with a bright pink door. As she stares at the painted wood, frightful memories return to her mind like cars colliding.

"I'm so scared! I don't know how I got here," her brother's muffled voice hysterically cries.

Chloe stands paralyzed. The young boy's frantic pleas emanating from behind the pastel-colored entrance assault her mind, and adrenaline fills her petite body as she struggles to focus. Her eyes graze the floor, and she sees the bedroom light turn on from beneath the door.

Kicking at the streaming light, she redirects her attention to the glittering sign nailed to the middle of the entry and reads what it says. "No boys allowed," Chloe mumbles.

Trying to overcome the horrible memories associated with the room, she closes her eyes to refocus on her brother. "Don't worry, I'm coming, Timothy," she says with hesitation. Still toting her duffle bag, she clutches it tighter and turns the doorknob. Slowly opening her eyes, she cracks the door and looks inside.

Immediately, she is met by her deepest fears. A folded pair of dingy pink pajamas sit upon her freshly made bed. Her racing mind nervously wonders who has prepared her room for her typical nighttime routine.

Hesitantly, she opens the door the remainder of the way to see if her mother is hiding inside. Seeing no sign of her parent, she rushes into her room and slams the door shut behind her. Offloading her ratty duffel bag onto the floor next to her nightstand, she neurotically searches for Timothy. "Timothy, are you in here?" she calls.

After looking under her bed, she opens each dresser drawer and peeks behind every piece of furniture in search of his hiding spot. "Where are you?" she anxiously asks.

Glancing toward her bedroom closet, she notices the door slightly ajar. "I promised I wouldn't leave you behind, so I have to find you," she states, using a calm inflection to hide her building fear.

Taking a step closer, she stops to listen and hears the echoing sound of children's laughter accompanied by the rustling of wire hangers against a wooden dowel.

Chloe sprints to the closet, excited to finally put an end to her little brother's disappearance. Excited by the prospect of the search being over, she hurls open the door. "This isn't funny, Timothy. We are not playing hide-and-seek," she says in an irritated tone.

Standing on her tiptoes, she searches every inch of the small space. "I'm serious. We have to get out of here before something bad happens!" she says, letting out a sizable exhale in frustration.

Believing that her brother may be playing a trick on her, she sneaks up on the single piece of hanging clothing. Yanking the dress scattered with a dingy floral pattern off its hanger, she looks behind it and finds that Timothy is not there.

She hears a loud bang and is startled by the door to the hidey-hole slamming shut behind her. Cowering in the corner underneath a rack of empty hangers, she panics. "Timothy, is that you?" she asks. Wrapping her hands tighter around her knees, she settles into a fetal position.

Reaching for a row of cubbies used for storing shoes, she eventually pulls herself back to her feet. Making her way to the closet exit, she knows she has no other choice than to open it.

Cautiously turning the knob, Chloe slowly enters the room and immediately realizes she is alone. Collapsing to her knees, she wonders who may have closed the door behind her. She pauses for a moment, hyper-focused on the white noise within the eerie quiet.

Suddenly, she is startled by the sound of distant, heavy footsteps in the hallway outside. She silently stands and tiptoes across the room. She lowers herself to the floor and looks under the bedroom's entrance to see if she can recognize the feet.

Peering underneath the door, she spots a familiar pair of pointed black heels, and her body stiffens. "You better not still be up," her mother shouts from the hallway.

As the woman ferociously knocks on the door, the loud thuds send deafening vibrations through the wood, and each unforgiving blow prompts Chloe's eyes to widen with fear.

"I thought I told you to go to bed," she yells. Knocking louder, she stomps her heels to get her daughter's attention.

"You better not be playing hide-and-seek with your brother again!" she shouts. Chloe panics at the thought of what her mother may do to her if she discovers her brother has gone missing on her watch.

"You know, I can hear you from all the way downstairs," she says. Realizing that she has been caught, Chloe quiets her breathing in hopes of not being discovered. "I know you can hear me in there," she says as she kicks the pink wooden entry.

Chloe scampers away from the door. The thought of what usually comes next in the narrative terrifies her, and she wants to escape.

Irritated by the lack of response from her daughter, her mother stomps her feet with rage. "Say something, you little brat! Don't make me repeat myself!" she screams.

Cowering further into her defensive shell, Chloe winces at each of her mother's loudening knocks. "Did you hear me?" the angry woman screeches at the top of her lungs.

The rattling sound of her mother jimmying the doorknob evokes panic to infiltrate Chloe's mind. "Yes, ma'am," she says with a trembling voice.

As her frozen mouth squeezes out the single words, the doorknob stops shaking. "OK, very good. Now, put on your pajamas and go to bed," her mother says. Trying not to make any extra noise, Chloe looks at the pajamas neatly folded on her bed and shivers.

"Your father will be home soon, and you know how he gets when everything is not on schedule," she says.

Hearing that her father would soon be home triggers Chloe to spring to her feet. Standing too quickly, she wobbles to her bed and misses the view of her mother's heels disappearing under the door. As her levitating feet float away, they morph into those of the Living Room Monster.

The absence of the sound of her mother's footsteps departing causes Chloe to shudder. Analyzing the pink pajamas, she holds them up to the light and recognizes that they are her mother's. Removing her clothes, but with her shoes still on, she reluctantly changes into the oversized pajamas and places her stained dress in her filthy duffel on the floor.

Chloe flips off the light switch in her room and sprints to climb into bed. Once inside the sheets, she pulls the blankets over her head to hide.

The covers reassure her for a moment until she hears the record player from the living room turn on, and a familiar song begins to play. She cups her ears with her hands to silence the melody and tightly closes her eyes, hoping to disappear.

"Please, please, make it stop," she pleads. Pinching her arm, she makes one last desperate attempt to wake herself up from the nightmare. "Wake up, Chloe. Come on, wake up," she says.

The sounds of heavy footsteps echo from the hallway like a beating bass drum, forcing her eyes to peel wide open. Focusing on the surrounding darkness, she hears muffled cries coming from Timothy's room next door, and it terrifies her.

"I'm in bed. I promise, Daddy, I'm in bed," Timothy sobs.

"No... no... no... please, you are hurting me," he whimpers.

A loud thud hits their conjoining wall, causing her to flinch. She desperately tries to hear what is happening next door, but her ears are met with silence. The echo of her brother's bedroom door shutting makes her afraid that she is next.

Heavy footsteps grow louder as they approach her room. Curling deeper under her blankets, she hears her bedroom door creak open. Tucked away and defenseless, she trembles as the sound of her father's boots move closer.

The mattress indents as he takes a seat, causing her to roll toward the twin bed's edge. Her body stiffens as she catches herself, stopping her momentum. Chloe is terrified to move as she is subjected to the caress of her father slowly petting her leg. Afraid to make a single peep, she pretends to be asleep, hoping he will be discouraged and leave.

"You know, your mother told me what happened at school today, and I hate to admit it, but I have to agree that you were being a bad girl," he says with a sick cockiness.

As he leans closer to his daughter, he quietly blows in her ear. "Do you think you were being a bad girl?" he whispers with a smile.

Angered by her lack of response, he rips away the covers to force eye contact. "No, sir! I swear I was good," she stammers.

Using a single hand to hide her face, she extends the other towards her father and sticks out her pinkie finger. "I pinkie swear," she quickly says.

He shakes his head to show his disapproval, laughing at his daughter's submissive display.

"Sir?" he asks with disgust, pouting to get her attention. "You know when you call me that, you make me feel old," he dejectedly mumbles, tapping her forehead with his pointer finger to the beat of each word.

"How many times do we have to have this conversation?" he asks. "You know, if you don't answer me, I will have to call the tickle monster to get you," he says with a low, gravelly, monster-like tone.

Lifting his hands above his head, he releases a deep roar. "Is that what you want?" he asks.

Unable to keep a straight face, he laughs. "I think you like to be tickled," he says with a smirk. Leaning closer, he tickles her neck. Squirming to escape, she shakes her head to get his hands away.

"Fine, then we'll have to try this again. How old am I?" He asks.

Holding up six fingers, Chloe pretends to guess his age with a number to please him. Happy with her answer, he kisses each of her extended digits.

"That's right, my baby girl," he shouts with a grin. Noticing her pull away, he forcefully cuddles her.

"Do you remember what daddies give little girls who are good?" he asks using a baby voice.

Trying to avoid eye contact, she raises her shoulders in response. Wanting to regain his daughter's attention, he flirtatiously taps the tip of her nose. She cringes at his advance.

Brushing off her rejection, he shrugs to mask his irritation. "Pull something like that again, and I might just have to take your nose," he says.

Immediately perking up, she covers her nose to protect it. Feeding off his daughter's frightened energy, he nudges her to watch him place a theatrical frown on his face. "Don't make me take your nose," he says with a mischievous laugh.

Watching her eyes follow his every movement leads him to feel powerful. Chuckling, he pats the front pocket of his dirty work shirt. "I'll just put your nose right here in my pocket," he says with excitement.

Continuing to feed off her fear, he releases a loud, clown-like cackle. "Baby girl, I've got to ask you a question," he whispers. "Do you know how hard life is when you can't smell?" he asks.

Reaching forward, he pinches Chloe's nose shut. Enjoying the spectacle of her inability to inhale a single sniff of air, he pauses before releasing his grip. Gasping, she wrestles with catching her breath. Still panicked from her inability to breathe through her nose, she begins to hyperventilate, which stimulates him to laugh hysterically.

Leaning closer to her, he touches his lips to her hair and whispers. "I will let you in on a little secret: if you just do what I say, you will never have to find out what it is like to lose your sniffer."

Remaining submissive, she timidly nods in agreement.

"Yes sir... um..." she says. Looking at the adjoining wall to Timothy's room, she hesitates to speak. "Dad... wh-where's Timothy?" she nervously stammers.

Sure that his daughter is switching the subject to avoid his flirtatious advance, he becomes angry. "Who?" he asks coldly.

Gaining more confidence, she takes a deep breath as she lowers her hands from her face. "My brother Timothy," she states timidly.

Hearing her mentioning the boy's name makes him jealous. "Oh, him... he's sleeping," he casually replies.

Gritting his teeth, he clenches his jaw to silence his annoyance. "What can I say, baby girl? Some kids can't be as perfect as you," he says with a careless shrug.

Hearing his negligent response regarding her brother's health makes her worry. "Can I see him?" she pleads.

Enjoying the spectacle of his daughter groveling prompts his confidence to skyrocket. "Why? So, you can fuck?" he asks.

Her father's vulgarity prompts her body to shrivel up into a self-conscious hunch. Loving the power, he continues. "Is that why you don't want to touch me?" he asks.

Tightly squeezing Chloe's shoulder, he finds arousal in his daughter's flinching. "Is that why you act like a prudish brat?" he shouts.

Throwing up his hands, he paces the room. "I mean, I always knew you two had a thing... I told your mother I never wanted a boy in the first place," he states.

Circling the room's perimeter, he takes out his anger by kicking her stuffed animals one by one, scattering them across the floor. Looking with fear at the flying plush toys, she imagines she could be next.

"I mean, the way you look at him...I should have known that you and your mom are more alike than not," he says.

She cries for him to stop. "Please, Daddy, stop. I love you. Can you please make sure Timothy's, OK?" she wails through the tears that stream down her cheeks.

Snickering at her pleas, he creepily tiptoes to the bedroom's exit. "He could be dead for all I care," he states calmly.

As he slams the door behind him, the horrific music ceases.

Grabbing the covers from her waist, she pulls them back over her head and cries. "I hate you, I hate you, I hate you!" she yells into the blanket.

Wiping the snot away from her nose, she gets out of bed and picks up a family photo sitting on her nightstand. "I won't let them hurt you, Timothy. I promise," she whispers reassuringly. Hugging the picture, she remembers all the great times spent with her brother. "Cross my heart and hope to die," she whimpers.

Sniffling to stop her tears, she takes the photo out of the frame. Holding it close, she traces the outline of each detail with her finger. She lovingly pauses on the image of Timothy's smiling face.

In the portrait, he is sitting at the dining room table, wearing a cheaply constructed cone-shaped birthday hat, and ogling a homemade cake with blue frosting that is positioned in front of him. Chloe sits next to him, wearing a matching party hat to celebrate his birthday. Standing behind the happy birthday boy is their mother with a fake smile plastered on her alcohol-glazed face.

Upon closer look, Chloe notices that the remaining chairs surrounding the table are empty, and her eyes droop with sympathy. "No matter what, we have each other," she says.

Wanting to reassure her brother trapped in the photo that he is loved, she gently places her fingers on his image. Closing

her eyes, she remembers the pivotal day and the warmth of
his toothy grin.

Chapter Six

HAPPY BIRTHDAY

The aroma of cake-baking wafts from the kitchen. Chloe refuses to open her eyes as she takes comfort from the smell.

Her moment of basking in the sensory experience is interrupted by realizing a weighty object resting on the top of her head. Raising her hands, she reaches for the mysterious item.

Her eyes dart open at the sound of Timothy's genuine laughter mere inches away. Looking next to her, she sees her brother wearing the same birthday hat from the photo in her bedroom.

The unsettling notion that she could relive another memory in real-time prompts her stomach to drop. She shudders as she analyzes the surrounding scene and realizes that Timothy is no longer dressed in the primped birthday outfit present in the photo. Instead, he is dressed in dirty clothes from their basement encounter earlier that day.

The scene is eerily off-putting to Chloe. Hesitantly, she looks down at her attire and panics at the sight of the pink pajamas still clinging to her body. Squinting, she analyzes each detail through dim lighting and quickly recognizes that this is not the same happy memory.

She moves her fingers back to the top of her head to feel the foreign object again. Realizing it is a party hat matching her brothers causes her to tremble with fear-laden anticipation. She watches the kitchen exit swing toward her, exposing her mother, who uses her back to push open the door.

Entering the dining area, she turns toward the children, showcasing the green welding apron hanging around her neck. Gripped in her hands is a blue frosted cake with four lit candles. The flickering flames help light her pathway through the darkened room as she walks towards the waiting duo. "Happy birthday to you," she says with a chipper tune.

Chloe refocuses her attention on Timothy to distract her from her feelings of nausea. The sight of his cheery face brings her a sense of wholeness—her brother's excitement on his memorable day triumphs over the worrisome idiosyncrasies that preoccupy her mind. Focusing on positive thoughts, she fixates on enjoying the moment. "Timothy!" Chloe says with elevated excitement.

Scanning over his dirty outfit, she checks his appearance to assure that he is not injured. "Where have you been?" she asks.

The flickering flames from the birthday candles move closer and catch her attention. Timothy claps his hands. "I looked for you everywhere. I was worried about you," Chloe quietly states.

Her words fall on deaf ears as he continues to focus on the cake with tunnel vision, like a horse wearing blinders. Timothy's energy seems different from earlier, and she swiftly becomes concerned. "It's my birthday, it's my birthday!" he shouts.

Clapping to the beat of his mother's slurred singing of the birthday song, he holds up four fingers, giggling as he turns to show Chloe. "I'm this many!" he says with excitement.

Clutching Timothy's tiny hand in between her fingers leads her eyes to well with tears. "Yes, you are, Timothy," she says.

The woman finally reaches the table, interrupting the siblings' loving moment. After setting the cake in front of the little boy, she mutters the rest of the song and stumbles to her seat. "Aren't you just the cutest?" she slurs with intoxication.

Barely able to keep her head lifted, she uses the table to support her weight. "Yes, you are, sweetie pie, yes, you are," the mother says in a baby voice.

Her inflection seems endearing to Timothy, and he smiles with an open grin, leaning forward to admire the cake positioned in front of him on the table.

"I would just die if you could be my baby boy forever," she states.

Reaching into her apron pocket, she pulls out a pint-sized half-empty bottle of whiskey and holds it in the air. "Hush, everyone—let's make a toast!" she says in a boastful tone. Bowing, she thanks the nonexistent audience sitting around the table for their preemptive silence.

Timothy thinks his mother is performing a birthday show and rapidly claps his hands to applaud her. Loving her attention, she nods her head to acknowledge him. Chloe sits quietly, watching her mother in dismay as she bows to her phantom audience and loses her balance.

She attempts to recoup the moment with a wink as she points the neck of her whiskey bottle at Timothy. "See, Chloe, that's why that one over there is my favorite," she declares.

Timothy laughs, still convinced that his mother is giving him a loving birthday performance. "That's right, I'm talking about the birthday boy!" she says with a smile.

Twirling the bottle in Timothy's direction, she places her hand on the table to stabilize herself and makes eye contact with Chloe. Pretending that the bottle of alcohol is the barrel of a gun, she closes one eye and looks down the neck to aim at her. "You should take notes," she shouts drunkenly.

Startled by a burp, Chloe watches as her mother uses the skin on her wrist to wipe her mouth and points the bottle back to Timothy. "He may resemble your scumbag father, but at least he has personality," she states. Each word smears into the next as she explains why she favors Timothy more.

Attempting to avoid her mother's hostility, Chloe nervously shrinks deeper in her seat and picks dirt from her nails.

Waving her hands like a magician performing a magic trick, the mother points to the cake in the middle of the table. "Who wants cake?" she shouts with overbearing amounts of vitality. Chloe looks at the lopsided cake and notices that the blue food coloring is splotchy.

Sitting patiently, Timothy shifts his weight and leans forward to look closer as he raises his hand with excitement, the wooden chair creaks. "Me! I do! I want cake!" he yells with a squeal. Unable to contain his glee, he taps his chest.

Still skeptical, Chloe analyzes the melting candles on the cake in front of them and looks towards her mother.

Making eye contact with her daughter, her mother laughs at her lack of appreciation for the back-breaking labor she performed in the kitchen. "So now you don't want food?" she says.

Using the back of her chair as a crutch, she rises to her feet. "You were practically begging yesterday and can starve for all I care. You're an ungrateful little bitch," she says.

As she dramatically rolls her eyes at her daughter, her body sways. Disallowing any time for a rebuttal, she abruptly staggers across the room and exits into the kitchen to grab serving utensils for the cake.

Seeing the door close behind her, Chloe leans towards Timothy and tries to plan an escape. "Timothy, listen to me," she whispers. She keeps watch for her mother's return and taps her brother, who remains eyeing the cake. He briefly glances at his sister to acknowledge that he is listening.

"I don't feel good about this. We need to get out of here," Chloe blurts. Shifting her vision to check that her brother is paying attention, she notices his expression of confusion.

"Something is not right," she says. Grabbing his knee, Chloe forces him to make direct eye contact with her. "Something feels bad," she whispers with a trembling voice.

The door to the kitchen opens, and Chloe quickly straightens her posture in her seat to assure that her mother would not become suspicious of her conspiring. Afraid of missing even a beat of her mother's disturbing antics, she refrains from blinking.

Watching her mother walk towards them, she notices that her hand clutches a camera instead of serving utensils. Seeing an odd familiarity with the approaching camera, she flashes back to the corrupt memory of the leaf photo. She recognizes that it is the same one her father had been using.

"Silly me!" the mother slurs. Holding the camera away from her face, she tries to figure out how to turn it on. Fiddling with each of the buttons, she finally concludes that she must remove the lens cap.

"I almost forgot to get a picture of the birthday boy before eating the cake," she says. Forcing a smile on her face, she adjusts the camera's settings.

Chloe takes a second to inspect her mother's disheveled appearance. Since returning from the kitchen, she notices her eyes are red from crying.

Her mother sniffles as she listens for the first click of the automatic timer to sound. Propping the camera up on a nearby shelf, she makes sure that the dining room table is in the frame for the photo.

Hearing the second click sound from the timer, she rushes to position herself behind the birthday boy for the picture. "OK, everyone, say cheese!" she shouts.

Timothy's eyes widen with excitement. "I love cheese!" he says while smiling.

Trying not to wince from the blinding flash, Chloe shifts her attention to look at her mother again. Still battling her blurred vision from the burst of light, she notices her mother's appearance shift as she wraps each of her arms around Timothy to hug him.

One by one, each of her fingers elongate, and her nails become discolored to match the Living Room Monsters.

The horrifying image triggers Chloe's heart to race, and she clutches her rib cage. Frantically rubbing her eyes, she attempts to erase the image. As she removes her hands from her face, she notices that her mother's fingers have returned to their original bony stature, and for a moment, she is relieved.

Her mother slowly turns to revel in the view of her daughter's deteriorating mental state. Smiling at her accomplishment, she joyfully skips to the shelf that the camera sits on. She picks it up and shifts her eyes back and forth between the photo screen and Chloe. "This photo sure would look better if I got an abortion the first time around," she states with a snarky tone.

She sets the camera back on the shelf and puts on a fake smile. She trips over her feet and crashes into the dining room table, making her way back towards the kids. Each layer of the cake wobbles from the impact as she uses the table to stabilize herself and laughs at both her own and the baked goods' buoyancy.

"Oh, yes, we were about to eat that cake," she says. Plopping her body onto the chair next to Timothy, she angrily glares at her daughter from across the table.

"Cake! I love cake!" Timothy howls with excitement.

Staring at the mounds of cold melted wax over sugary frosting causes Timothy to twitch eagerly.

Leaving her glare locked on her daughter, she raises her bare hand to the ceiling and dives it into the blue frosted cake. Scooping up a handful, she splats it on the filthy wooden table in front of her son.

The gesture horrifies Chloe. Finding her daughter's reaction entertaining, she briefly breaks eye contact to take a swig of whiskey.

"I'm going to share a fun fact with both of you," she says. Ignoring Timothy, she leans over the table and directs her words towards Chloe. "Did you know that when prisoners are on death row, they get to choose a last meal?" she asks with an inappropriate chuckle.

She mimics slitting her own throat with the hand covered with blue frosting smudges. "Before they croak!" she screams with a howl while reveling in her words bringing terror to her daughter's eyes.

Absent from the conversation, Timothy admires the cake that still lays smashed in front of him.

"That just gave me a brilliant idea. Let's go around the table and share what we would choose to eat for our last meal," the mother says. As she slurs each word, she claps her hands to signify that the children are in for a treat. "This will be such a fun game!" she says.

Glaring at her daughter, she removes all signs of happiness from her face. "Chloe!" she shouts. Clearing her throat, she prepares for her next round of torment. "My little honey bunny, why don't you start us off?" she asks with sarcastic endearment.

Chloe's vocal cords freeze with anxiety. "What would your last meal be?" her mother asks.

Seeing that his mother is not paying attention, Timothy sticks his pointer finger into the cake and skims the frosting.

As his finger is halfway across the cake's surface, his mother's head neurotically snaps up to look. Deeming her son's behavior barbaric, she slams her fist against the table's surface to make him stop. Chloe flinches from the noise.

"Goddammit, Timothy! Have some fucking manners!" she screams with a disgusted look on her face.

Frightened by his mother's harsh tone, he swiftly wipes his finger clean on his dirty shirt as he looks towards the ground.

"Yes, momma," he replies. Trying to avoid eye contact, he nervously fidgets in his chair. "I'm sorry, momma," he says.

After mocking her son's apprehensive words with a miming hand, their mother directs her rage back to Chloe. "Answer me now!" she says. Spitting as she over articulates each word, she finds enjoyment in watching her daughter cower.

Sinking deeper into the worn seat, Chloe stammers, struggling to form a complete sentence. "Um... um," she stutters.

Placing the bottle back in her apron, her mother slams the table with her clutched fist. "Goddammit, Chloe, use your words. It's not that fucking hard to speak... Jesus!" she states.

Both children stare at their mother in silence. "Just pick something—anything!" she shouts.

Chloe's eyes dart as she frantically thinks of an answer. "I guess I would have... pizza?" she says, ducking her head in anticipation of a violent reaction from her mother.

Lunging at her daughter, her mother catches her balance on the edge of the table. The cake wobbles in coordination with her roaring laughter. "Pizza? You would choose pizza?" she questions in a demeaning tone. Pushing herself away from the table, she rolls her eyes to signal her disapproval as she paces the room.

"You have to be joking... you get one last meal, and you would choose pizza? What a dumbass!" she says.

Throwing up her hands, she declares that she is surrounded by stupidity. "Go figure," she states sarcastically.

Reaching back into her apron, she snatches the partial bottle of whiskey and takes a shot. Placing the bottle back, she laughs at the sight of her daughter starting to cry. "You are just like your father!" she says with a snicker. Sniffling her running nose, Chloe avoids eye contact with her mother.

Irritated by her daughter's non-confrontational response, her mother moves to her next child for a more fulfilling answer. Giving Timothy her undivided attention, she points her finger at his quivering head. "OK, birthday boy. Now it's your turn," she says.

Moving closer to her son, she turns her head to the side to give his words her full attention. "What would you choose?" she asks.

Clapping with excitement, he stares at the birthday cake splattered on the tabletop. "Cake!" he shouts gleefully.

Filled with a sense of accomplishment, she journeys back to her chair and calmly takes a seat. "Well, I guess today is your lucky day, kiddo! Eat up!" she says with uncharacteristic exuberance.

Chloe questions her mother's odd happiness. A terrible epiphany consumes her mind regarding the birthday cake ingredients, and her body language cannot conceal her assumptions.

Reading her daughter's cues, her mother dramatically rolls her eyes. "Come on, Chloe, give me a fucking break. You think I'm going to poison the birthday boy?" she indignantly asks.

Both continue to watch Timothy eat the cake with his dirty hands. She mockingly sticks her tongue out at Chloe as he consumes the last bite.

"See, you little freak? I told you so," she says with a snicker. After chugging the last bit of whiskey, she places the empty bottle back in her apron and slowly shakes her head.

"He would have been dead by now," she murmurs with a belch.

Redirecting her attention to her son, she softens her tone and asks, "How's the cake, Tim, Tim? YOU know I would never do anything to you, my precious little gift from God."

Licking the last bit of frosting from his lips, he smiles in response. Exhausted from pretending to care, their mother scoots her chair away from the table and slumps to get comfortable in her seat. Resting her head against the top of the chair's wooden back, she closes her eyes to stabilize the room. She fumbles in her apron pocket for a pack of cigarettes and pulls a single cig from the box, places it in her mouth, and grabs for her lighter.

Looking at the empty chairs around the table, Chloe becomes curious. "Where's Dad?" she asks.

Lighting her cigarette, her mother takes a deep inhale before opening her eyes to look towards the empty chair where her husband usually sits. "That has to be a joke," she says without expression.

Fixing her posture to address her daughter, she sits up in her seat. Noticing her mother's shifted position prompts Chloe to realize that she has made a grave mistake by speaking out. As her mother leans forward to show her dominance, she sinks deeper into her seat. "I mean, I guess I can't expect anything less from having a child who is a chronic liar," her mother says. Finishing the last puff of her cigarette, she extinguishes the smoldering butt in a remaining bit of cake.

Trying not to cry, Chloe fights away her oncoming tears by clenching her jaw. "I'm not a liar," she says.

She is fueled by disbelief at her daughter's rebuttal, and her mother slowly stands up from her chair. "So, if you didn't lie, I assume you just wanted to ruin my life when you told all of those outlandish stories to your teacher?" she says.

Seething with hatred, her face turns red. "You just want to kill any chance I have at happiness," her mother states. She watches her daughter grow uncomfortable as she spews vile accusations.

Chloe scrambles to defend herself and protect her brother. "I didn't lie, momma!" Chloe sobs. Trying to stick up for herself, she looks at Timothy, who is still distracted by the remnants of the cake.

Belligerent from the alcohol, her mother crawls on top of the table. "I just have to ask you one question, sweetie," she says.

Winking at Chloe, she crawls a little closer to establish intimacy. "You know, like, girl to girl," she says with a smirk. Uncomfortable with the conversation, Chloe tries to escape by scooting further away in her chair.

"How did you like it?" her mother asks.

Hearing her mother's words confirms her greatest fear. She now knows that her mother is aware of her traumatic situation, but instead of standing up for her, she condones her father's molesting behavior.

Waiting for Chloe's response makes her mother's blood boil and triggers her to hop off the table and throw a chair across the room. The little girl stares in panic as her mother grabs a butcher knife from a nearby buffet counter. Petrified, she observes her mother playing with the blade.

"I mean, was that your plan all along, to just waltz into this world and take my place?" she says.

Not wanting to provoke her mother further, Chloe remains silent.

"I'm used to your father claiming I'm crazy, but for you to fuck me over like this—I'd say that takes the cake for betrayal," she says.

Recalling each time her husband chose Chloe over her fills her with hatred, but the sight of her crying daughter makes her laugh as she continues to blame her for everything.

"I didn't say anything, I swear, momma," the little girl pleads.

Motioning with the knife in her hand, her mother summons her daughter to come to her. Pretending not to understand, Chloe refuses to move from her seat.

Her mother smiles at Timothy. "Timothy, let's play a fun birthday game," she says. Hearing that someone wants to play a game on his birthday makes Timothy excited.

"How many boo-boos do you think your sissy should get?" she asks as her lips form a sinister grin.

With his face still smeared with blue frosting, Timothy looks at his mother's hand, still holding the knife, and panics. Entertained by watching her children squirm, she focuses her glare back at Chloe. "I'll give you to the count of three to get over here before I punish you both," she says.

As she twirls the knife like a baton, she commends herself on her clever ultimatum and laughs. Fear that her mother may hurt Timothy prompts Chloe to jump to her feet. Squeezing her brother's arm, she attempts to let him know everything will be okay.

Then, taking a deep breath, Chloe reluctantly turns and walks towards her. "Now, that wasn't so bad, was it?" she says with a demonic cackle. Hesitating to answer, Chloe shakes her head and fixates on the swinging knife that may determine her fate.

Still deeply confused by the transpiring events, Timothy's eyes well with tears. "Don't hurt her, momma!" he cries.

Showing no sympathy for her son's emotions, their mother snaps her fingers to shoo him away. "Just eat your cake, baby, and enjoy your last moments," she unemotionally replies.

As she takes a nervous gulp, Chloe motions for Timothy to be quiet. Moving another step forward, she holds up three fingers behind her back to get her brother's attention.

Becoming impatient with her daughter's slow movement, their mother takes an enormous step in her direction. "You think you can just ruin my life, huh?" she asks.

Locking her knees, Chloe tries to stop from shaking and puts down one finger behind her back. Noticing his sister's signal, Timothy's eyes widen.

"You think you can be the woman of the house?" their mother screams. The thought of her cheating husband fuels her enraging energy.

Putting down a second finger behind her back, Chloe shakes her head. "No, momma," she stammers.

Taking another step closer, her mother smiles at her daughter's lack of words. "Since we're having this fun little bonding moment, I'm going to fill you in on another secret: I never wanted you," her mother states with an inappropriate chuckle.

Feeding off the impact of her cruel words, she continues louder, "Or maybe it's not a secret."

Chloe's fists clench, and her muscles tense as rage floods her body from the years of her mother's abuse. As she places her last finger down behind her back, she lets out a guttural scream. Charging her mother's legs, she ambushes her, throwing off her precarious balance.

The impact of Chloe's small tackle causes her mother's arms to flail. Dropping the knife, she continues to stumble to the floor, and the blade's obscure position slices her leg.

Seeing her brief window of opportunity to escape, Chloe runs to the bloody knife lying next to her mother and picks it up. Looking at Timothy, she snaps her fingers to wake him from his state of shock and points to the exit.

"Now, Timothy... go!" she screams. Using the blade of the butcher knife, she directs him to get up. "Run!" she shouts.

Chloe's scream jolts Timothy from his trancelike state, he runs for the door, and she follows closely behind. As she witnesses him desperately try to open the locked living room entrance, her stomach drops.

Then, the lights in the dining room suddenly shut off, leaving the children in complete darkness.

Ready to defend them, Chloe clutches the knife tighter in her fist. Flailing her empty hand in the darkness, she connects with her brother's shirt, grabs it, and pulls him towards the kitchen door. Whispering under her breath, she makes a wish to keep them safe.

Pushing on the door with her shoulder, it opens, and the children rush inside the kitchen to take shelter.

Chapter Seven

THE KITCHEN MONSTER

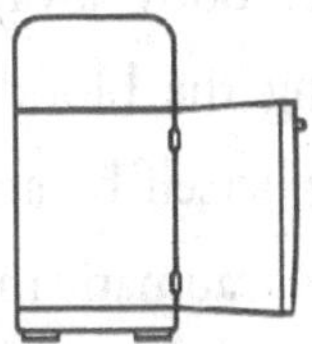

Entering the room hastily, Chloe sternly moves Timothy in front of her and pushes him across the room to safety. With her brother secured, she shifts her attention to safeguarding the door from the horror of a mother. Nervous about approaching the kitchen's only entrance, Chloe takes a moment to gather her courage. After inhaling a large gulp of air, she pivots her body to face the door behind her.

Staring at the metal lock, she reorients her racing mind and darts across the room to turn the latch. The sound of clicking metal comforts her and provides a sense of relief that she has further kept her brother out of harm's way.

Finally able to catch her breath, she inhales the aroma of the kitchen. The lingering smell of cake baking triggers a comforting sensation that infiltrates her mind. She closes her eyes and desperately tries to use the scent to envision a happy feeling of home that only resides in her dreams.

The excruciating pain of her trembling hand makes it impossible for her to reach her dream state, and she is forced back to the seriousness of their predicament. Analyzing the root cause of her situational pain, she loosens her nervously clenched fist after realizing that her hand's constricting grip around the knife's handle is causing her knuckles to turn stark white.

The sight of fresh blood dripping from the knife's edge causes her to shudder. Trying to avoid the gruesome spectacle, she turns her body away from the blade and extends her arm, placing the bloody knife on the closest countertop. Distracting herself by analyzing the tiny details of the area, she wipes the traumatic image of her mother's leg sliced to the bone from her memory.

As she scans the room that provides them temporary shelter, she immediately notices the truly appalling condition of the kitchen. Excessive amounts of baking supplies that her mother had used to craft the infamous birthday cake litter each square inch of the kitchen's floor and counters. Flour and frosting mask the repulsive nature of what lies beneath their chaotic cover.

Weeks' worth of dishes speckled with putrid green hues fills the sink and oven cavities. Pungent odor's of decaying animal flesh and sour milk waft through the sugary smells, creating a sickening sweet smell of decay. Every grout line is filled past the level of the porcelain tile with unidentifiable particles of food and filth.

Repulsed by the putrid mess, Chloe turns her attention away and focuses on Timothy. She immediately notices a pan precariously teetering on the off-white tile counter above his head. She watches nervously as the heavy cast iron sways on the porcelain's rounded edge.

Observing her brother's state of shock, she takes matters into her own hands. Running to protect him, she stands on her tiptoes and attempts to nudge the baking dish to a safer position. However, not tall enough to have a clear view of the countertop, she is oblivious to the number of items that clutter its surface. Her aggressive movements cause an avalanche of baking supplies and soiled dishes to fall to the tiled floor. Startled by the loud sound of crashing pans and shattering porcelain, she ducks to the ground in panic and covers her ears.

While his sister cowers in fear, Timothy becomes intrigued by the novel items surrounding him. Perking up at the sight of the multitude of baking materials scattered on the tiled surface, he spots a small, opened box with a cartoon rat stamped on the front. As he picks up the carton to look at the comic strip-like drawing, white powder sprinkles on him.

Timothy inspects the image and giggles at the fossilized mouse lying on its back, believing it to be napping. "Look, Chloe, it's a mouse, just like the fairy tale," he says, squealing with excitement. Sticking his fingers inside the box, he plays with the white substance as if it is snow.

Slowly rising from the floor, Chloe glances over the small carton that her little brother finds so entertaining. When she realizes that the picture he finds amusing is that of a dead mouse and that the snowy white substance is rat poison, her body fills with terror. Panicking, she runs towards him and swats the package away from his hands.

As the flying powder coats the floor, Timothy begins to cry. "You can't touch that!" Chloe shrieks. The series of events frighten Timothy.

Watching his teardrops cascade down his blue frosted cheeks and onto the sprinkled rat poison, she notices the mixture turn into a paste. The image of the frosting-like consistency induces her imagination to run wild. She slowly looks at the scattered birthday cake baking supplies and panics.

Realizing that her dread-filled suspicion has terrified her brother, she tries to contain her racing thoughts. Pushing aside her deep-seated fears, she cradles his head to comfort him. "Shh... it's okay... you are okay," she whispers.

She hopes to soothe her brother and convince herself that he will be okay through her calming tone and word choice. Combing through Timothy's greasy curls with her undernourished fingers, she sits in silence and enjoys the peaceful moment, holding him close to her chest. "We are going to be alright," she whispers.

Chloe wraps her arms around Timothy and hugs him tighter. Using the bare palm of her hand, she tries to wipe the leftover blue frosting from his face. Noticing that the food coloring has stained his skin, she tries rubbing with more pressure.

"It's fine, Timothy. I'm not mad. You didn't know any better," she says.

Observing Timothy's eyelids beginning to droop as he becomes drowsy, she sings a lullaby and rocks him back and forth to calm him further. Comforted by his sister's melodic words, he closes his eyes and falls asleep.

Pounding sounds from their mother's aggressive knocks ruin the tranquil moment. Chloe flinches at the loud echoes, and the unrelenting hammering triggers Timothy's eyes to dart open.

"Please, children, open the door. I didn't mean any of that stuff I said earlier," their mother says.

Huddled on the kitchen floor, the children glare at the locked door and tremble with fear.

"You both know that I would never hurt you," their mother shouts. Catching herself, she softens the hardness of her voice. "I know you're both in there. Come on, Tim Tim, open the door for Mommy."

Confident that her manipulation will prove successful, she waits in silence for the children to respond. Met with no reply, she becomes furious and angrily bangs on the door with her feet and fists.

The crazed woman's aggression triggers Chloe's survival instinct, and she looks across the room towards the knife resting on the counter. As each knock grows louder, she prepares for the worst-case scenario. Panicked that her mother will break through the entry, she quietly crawls towards the weapon.

"Chloe, you little bitch, open the fucking door!" their mother shrieks through the latched wood.

Without warning, the screaming stops, and the sound of a demonic cackle and rapidly departing healed footsteps replaces the temporary silence. Relieved to arrive at the counter's edge, Chloe finds comfort leaning her back against the cabinet base. While keeping her body low and still, she cautiously reaches onto the flat surface and blindly rummages for the knife with one hand. She pushes her ear up against the adjoining wooden door to listen for any sign of her mother's movement.

Hearing the scratching needle from the living room record player turn on prompts her to freeze and firmly latch her grip onto the knife's handle. A familiar melody plays in the distant room and sends shivers down her spine.

"Fine! Do you want to play? Let's play!" their mother states.

The sound of their mother's screeching voice causes Chloe to wince. Pushed by her will to stay alive, she pulls the bloody knife from the counter with her clenched fist and turns to look at her brother.

"It's okay, Timothy," she calls across the room. Holding her empty hand out in his direction, she tries to comfort him.

Chloe panics as the fluorescent bulbs start to flicker. Then, without warning, the kitchen lights shut off, leaving the children in complete darkness. Bit by bit, the main door of the refrigerator near Timothy slowly cracks open, allowing the dim light inside to escape and cut through the lightless space.

All at once, boiling black tar begins oozing from the inside compartment, exiting through the unsealed opening. As it seeps onto the floor, the substance melts each tile one by one.

Frightened by the abstractness of the scene unfolding, Timothy looks desperately to Chloe for help. With no time to waste, she signals her brother to crawl towards her. Following his sister's instruction, he hastily slides on his knees in her direction. She extends a hand as he reaches her feet and pulls him up next to her.

Staring at the morphing refrigerator, they watch with horror as the top freezer door swings open, releasing demonic crimson lighting. Large, pointed teeth resembling sharpened icepicks sprout from the freezer's shelves, and the ominous red light bounces off their porcelain finish as the pearly whites gain size. Reflected light illuminates a pair of large gelatinous eyes with small glowing marble pupils emerging from the ice tray drawer. The diabolical eyes glare across the room, fixating their menacing stare on the children.

Timothy hides behind his big sister for protection. Burrowing his face in her pink pajamas, he misses the sight of the produce shelf in the main compartment, slowly opening to release a long, forked, serpent-like tongue.

As the tar creeps closer to their feet, Chloe watches each floor tile that the substance touches disintegrate. Frightened that her feet will be next, she pushes Timothy to take a step backward. "We're not afraid of you!" she screams, clutching the knife tighter in preparation to defend them.

The fridge malevolently growls at her threat and bares its pick-like fangs. Its tongue snakes wildly in the air as the monstrous fridge moves closer to the children. Frightened by the guttural sounds of the beast, Timothy tightens his grip around his sister's legs.

Seeing it fast approaching, Chloe frenziedly swings the butcher knife in front of her for protection. The vicious glare from the fridge's familiar marble eyes sparks her to panic. Unsure of what to do next, she faces her brother to calm him.

"It's okay, Timothy," she says.

Redirecting her tone, she tries to mask the distressed timbre of her voice while calming her brother by comparing their dire situation to a familiar childhood game. "Look, Timothy, that thing over there is just playing a game, so we have to play," she says.

Staring past his sister, Timothy anxiously fixates on the creature oozing darkened tar. Although he is horrified, he reluctantly forces himself to nod.

Chloe takes one last moment, swiftly scanning the kitchen for another way for them to escape. Not finding any other viable option, she carries on with her explanation. "Remember that hot lava monster game we always used to play with dad?" she quickly asks.

Shaking off the traumatic memory of the abusive repercussions that occurred when they fell into the lava during their father's version of the game, she stares blankly at the bubbling tar. Timothy becomes engulfed by fear, and his body freezes. Using her knifeless hand, she shakes his shoulder to get him to focus.

"Okay, look, Timothy," she states as she points the tip of the knife's blade towards the snarling fridge, "that's the lava monster."

Glancing in the blade's direction, he nods, and his eyes widen at the sight of the terrifying entity. Moving the knife from the direction of the fridge, she points it at the boiling tar on the floor. "And that's the lava," she states.

Chloe tries to maintain her composure while searing heat from the approaching tar singes her blonde strands and chars her face. Using the back of her hand, she wipes the dripping sweat away from her forehead and points the knife towards the kitchen counter. "We've got to get up there to escape the hot lava, and we gotta go now!" she states urgently.

Chloe opens the cupboard door under the kitchen sink exposing the shelf as a stepping stool, and signals Timothy to hurry. Reaching for his foot and using what energy she has left, she boosts him onto the countertop.

He wiggles around, pushing clutter out of his way and kicking trash to the floor to create enough room for his temporary existence on the elevated space. He looks down at his sister, concerned that she will not join him, and he will be left to survive alone.

Knowing that she has no one to do the same for her, she looks for other ways to get onto the tall counter. She quickly opens a silverware drawer and two others that sit diagonally from the sink's cupboard. Starting with the sink's cabinet ledge, she begins her precarious ascent. She climbs to the first drawer, then the second, and suddenly pauses on the third.

Concerned by the proximity of the demonic monster's cackling voice, she stops to look behind her and stares in horror as each ear-piercing screech of the monsters' violent orchestration brings the kitchen to life. Bit by bit, each drawer is summoned by the evil call of the beast to dislodge themselves from their cubbies.

Frantically clinging onto the slippery lip of the smooth tile countertop, Chloe tries to find solid footing by stepping onto the open silverware drawer. The drawer disappears from beneath her foot, and she scrambles to get a better grip on the top of the counter to hoist herself up. Then, crawling next to the sink bowl, she sits to catch her breath as she watches the silverware drawer melt into the black tar abyss.

The fridge demonically cackles with laughter, trying to burn the children with its tongue, splashing boiling tar in their direction. Each splash barely misses the sibling's limbs as the monster's aim gains accuracy.

Timothy's eyes gape open in terror as he watches a speck of smoldering tar burn a hole in a cabinet next to him. Planting his hands against the surrounding tile, he refuses to move.

Desperate to keep them both alive, Chloe hurries towards her brother to escape the flinging tar. "Crawl forward, Timothy! Crawl!" she shouts.

Listening to his sister, he tries his best to hurry further away from the fridge. His kicking feet scatter baking supplies and dirty dishes into the boiling tar.

Chloe tries to stay close behind him but becomes separated by swinging cabinet doors. Dodging each animated shelf, she watches in horror as cast-iron baking pans instantly disintegrate upon touching the boiling ooze. Ashy smoke is all that remains of their once-tangible existence.

Having no other option than to inhale the contaminated, smoke-filled air, they cough spasmodically from the toxins. Chloe attempts to limit her lungs' noxious intake by plugging her nose and puffing out her cheeks to hold her breath. Releasing an exhalation, she takes in shallow amounts of necessary oxygen—just the minimum needed to remain conscious and resume her crawl.

The fridge's nefarious cackles get louder, causing the kitchen's demonic chaos to escalate vigorously.

Scouring the remaining shelving doors that lie in front of her for movement, Chloe spots a cabinet that begins to shake near her brother.

Timothy sees the terror in her stare, and he tries to gain comfort by fixating his eyes on hers. As the cabinet shakes more violently, Timothy's fear escalates, causing him to scoot backward blindly to escape.

Seeing that he is not paying attention to his surroundings overwhelms Chloe with panic. Using the last bit of air remaining in her lungs, she shouts to warn him of the oncoming obstacle.

The sound of his sister's strained voice compels Timothy to become alert just as the cupboard door flies open and a series of dinner plates ejects towards the children. The breaking porcelain resonates like glass-filled bombs and causes Timothy to wince.

He slowly turns and looks toward a shattered plate that almost hit his fragile skull. His body freezes, and he covers his small ears with his hands to stop his eardrums from ringing. Overwhelmed by the loud sounds of the breaking glass, he begins to hyperventilate.

"Breathe! It's okay, breath!" Chloe yells over the screeching chaos. Witnessing her brother's panic worsen, she feeds off his exuding fear and subconsciously joins in on the emotional frenzy. Trying to re-center herself, she recognizes Timothy's asthma attack limits his ability to respond. The severity of the situation sparks immense amounts of adrenaline to pump through her veins, prompting her to crawl faster.

Observing that the distance between her and her brother is not decreasing, she becomes alarmed. She watches in panic as the kitchen counter's tiling stretches as if in a carnival funhouse mirror, and the surrounding atmosphere spins around her like an elongated orbit. Her peripheral vision blurs like the sensation of having a severe migraine.

Struggling to regather her eyes' focus, she experiences a dark tunnel vision as she attempts to maintain sight of Timothy. Squinting to look for her brother on the opposite end of the skewed countertop, she can only discern outlined motions of him struggling.

Ignoring the surrounding distractions, she shoves the debris in her path out of the way as she treks forward. She is trapped in hell as every infinitesimal movement turns into a slow-motion bout of torture. Each of her limbs becomes heavy, like swimming through a vat of hardened molasses.

Timothy notices that his sister's pace contradicts her words from earlier, and he fears that she may choose to abandon him just like everyone else in his life. Swinging his arms in the air, he tries to get her attention for help one last time, and when he sees no improvement in her pace, his trembling body's energy switches to survival mode. Slapping the surrounding tile, he frantically hits everywhere in the vicinity for his inhaler. The immense friction and heat cause his tiny fists to become raw.

Unable to locate his life-saving device, he fixates his attention on each dwindling breath. Falling onto his back, he looks at the ceiling, and his grim reality feeds his fear of dying as his body continues to endure the stress of suffocation and his eyes unnaturally bulge from his skull. Any ounce of hope that his sister will save him diminishes as he clings to his memories for guidance.

Violently hitting his jugular, he attempts to use his tiny fingers to stop the sensation of drowning, but instead of helping ease the situation, the severe trauma sprouts bruises across his delicate skin. Finding no relief from the only method he could remember his father using to cure his asthma leaves him mentally defeated.

The fear of his father's disappointment overtakes his fear of death. Allowing his desperation for parental love to take over, the child believes that his failure to save himself correlates to his lack of effort. Performing one last valiant attempt to prove his worthiness of survival, he uses a tight fist to strike his neck harder, and the blunt force crushes his trachea. Frantically wrapping his hands around the front of his neck, the concavity of his airway vibrates as oxygen escapes into his throat. As it becomes harder to fight for coherence, his terrified mind slowly drifts away.

"Hold on! I'm coming, Timothy!" Chloe screams.

Going against the turbulence that confines her causes Chloe's stiffened joints to shake. A single tear rolls down her paralyzed face as she screams with frustration. Frozen in a mid-crawl position, her dry eyes watch a single teardrop fall into the rising tar that is nearing the counter's edge.

Startled by a loud knocking sound, she shifts her gaze to the kitchen door. "Knock, knock!" her mother yells from the dining room.

She tries to ignore her harassing words. Looking down at her hands, she notices that the shrieking timbre of her mother's voice has allowed them to unhinge, and, with new momentum, she inches closer to help her brother.

"You hungry now?" their mother asks. Her devious cackle catches Chloe's attention, and she looks to the kitchen door.

Silently begging for help, her eyes fill with tears as her brother's tiny body seizes. The convulsions worsen, causing one of his hands to flail into the center of a wooden cabinet uncontrollably.

The horrible sound of his cracking bone prompts Chloe's state of slow motion and tunnel vision to dissipate. All at once, her motor functions return, and for the first time, she can accurately see the full extent of her brother's deteriorating state. She notices the color of his smooth face shifting to match the blue frosting stains that still surround his darkened lips.

"It will be our little secret, Chloe! You and me," her mother says from behind the locked door.

Shoving aside a spatula, Chloe rids her path of the last obstacle in her way to reach her brother. She scurries around his tiny, twitching feet and desperately searches his seizing body for his inhaler.

"I can make all of this go away," she states. Knowing of her children's close-knit relationship, she attempts to use it to manipulate her daughter.

Running out of time to find his inhaler, Chloe becomes hysterical as she watches her little brother's life dwindle in front of her. Her desperation to save her brother and end the chaos urges her to consider her mother's offer. Setting her knife down on the counter beside her, she cradles his head to comfort him. Shifting her eye line to the door, she realizes she must decide.

"We can even pinkie promise," her mother says. Sensing the extent of her daughter's desperation, she continues to lure her by feeding off her deep love for her brother. "What do you say?" she asks.

Chloe becomes entranced by the support that her mother's voice seems to bring as she rocks her brother. Momentarily transfixed by her mother's web of prompting tones, she causes her hand to leave Timothy's head behind and her fifth digit to rise.

As the weight of her brother's head hits her lap, she closes her eyes to escape. "You are not real! Stop it! Go away!" Chloe shrieks.

She tries to drown out both her mother's voice and the horrible nightmare with all her might. The strength of her scream breaks her cryptic trance, and she is faced with the grim reality of Timothy's limp body on top of her.

Before acknowledging the certainty of her brother's lifeless face, she takes a deep breath to calm herself. Racked with guilt, she looks down on her brother's dead body and cries uncontrollably. A single tear falls onto Timothy's face and settles within one of his dimples. "Timothy, breathe," she sobs.

Leaning over his frail frame, she places a flat palm on each of his cheeks, then clutches his head to gaze into his bloodshot eyes and weeps. "We are safe. She can't get us. I swear, if you wake up, everything is going to be okay," she pleads.

Heartbroken, she begs for forgiveness for her failure to save him. Embracing Timothy's asphyxiated corpse, she attempts to give him the affection she knows he deserved but never received from their neglectful parents. Her emotional pain becomes unbearable, and she collapses her entire body's weight onto Timothy. Her wailing screams rival the tenacity of the aggressive knocking, which continues to grow louder.

Convinced that she is beyond her breaking point, she closes her swollen eyes to wait for the tar to boil her flesh and cook the heart that she no longer wishes to use. Anticipating the excruciating pain, she seals her eyes tighter and releases a final, mournful howl.

As the last of the cry leaves her lips, the glow of flickering lights drifts through her thin eyelids, and she instantly realizes that the treacherous music has stopped. Reluctantly, she forces herself to open her eyes and finds the kitchen restored to its original state. The fridge now only serves its legitimate purpose of storing food.

Wiping the tears from her face, she discovers she is huddled into a small ball. Slowly uncoiling herself, she notices that, along with all the baking supplies and clutter disappearing, Timothy has as well. Looking around, she sees that the only item of familiarity left is the bloody butcher knife still sitting next to her.

"Timothy, where are you?" she shouts. She scans the echoing room, thinks back to the nightmare, and becomes hysterical. A wave of anxiety sweeps over her body.

"Stay where you are, Timothy. Just stay there, and I will find you, I promise!" she yells. Knowing she has no time to waste, she snatches the butcher knife from the counter and hops down.

As her feet touch the floor, copious amounts of adrenaline kick in. Remembering that her mother may be waiting outside of the only exit which leads to the dining room, she runs around the kitchen to search for alternate escape routes.

Spotting a large, grated square vent on the far side of the room, she knows it is her only option. Setting aside her fearful thoughts, she inhales a large gulp of air before locking out her trembling legs.

"I can't let anything bad happen to you. I can't," Chloe says under her breath.

Her fingers nervously fidget around the knife's handle, and, using her words, she channels confidence to steady her hand. "No matter what, I will protect you," she states with newfound tenacity.

Running to the vent, she uses the knife's pointed tip to jimmy under each side of the metal to pry it open. Taking a moment to investigate the vent's dark abyss, she knows what she must do to save her brother, and she quickly climbs inside.

Chapter Eight

THE VENT

The inside of the pitch-black vent contains a fog-like film that makes the murky ambiance a shade of gray. Copious amounts of cobwebs cover every corner.

As she crawls through the square-shaped tunnel, the air conditioning system turns on, accompanied by the sound of loud clinking reverberations. Strong smells of mildew pelt Chloe's nose.

Fumbling her way through the dark shaft, she finds which direction to move forward by touching the sides of the air ducts. By mentally noting the details of the tunnel as they relate to the number of crawls she has taken, she can reassure herself that she is not trapped in the horrid claustrophobic escape from the kitchen.

She forms a mantra that she mutters under her breath to convince herself that she is brave enough to continue. "I'm not scared of monsters," she whispers.

An unexpected cobweb sticks to her face, providing a further reminder of the traumatic series of events that she had experienced in the kitchen. Her body shudders as she looks over her shoulder at the passage behind her.

"I'm not scared of monsters," she states, slightly louder than before.

As she masks the residual fear that plagues her body, she realizes that the direction she has crawled from appears different from before. She tries to focus her eyes on the rays of light from the kitchen ventilation opening to get a better look and realizes that the grated lid is closed. She gulps air to squash the burning thought that smothers her mind: who may have shut the vent's lid behind her?

Redirecting herself to continue forward, she forces her body to turn around and crawl deeper into the dark abyss. "I'm not scared of monsters," she says.

She directs her knees to inch forward. Without warning, she is startled by the sound of a door's creaking hinges echoing through the ventilation ducts, causing her petite body to jump. Hearing the abnormal sound infiltrate the tunnel generates a look of terror that engulfs her eyes. Scanning her dark surroundings, she tries to find the direction from which the screeches originated.

Her search leads her to notice harsh speckles of light in the distance. They project from the slats of another vent opening like a starry night onto the adjacent wall made of tin. Enticed by the pattern, she picks up the pace of her crawling to investigate. As she gets closer to the escaping light, she notices that she can hear a muffled male voice near the mysterious illumination.

Each inflection of the conversation faintly infiltrates the layer of protection from the air ducts, which seem like sturdy prison bars, and she stops crawling for a moment to listen.

Unable to identify the familiar voice, she makes her way to the grated opening to take a closer look, and her heart sinks. She quickly gains bearings on her location as she peers through the slatted opening. The vent overlooks the living room, and her father has arrived home through the front door, creating the mysterious creak.

Seeing her father's alive-and-well face paralyzes Chloe with fear. As she gives in to her frozen stance, she allows her eyes to watch the scene unwind in silence.

The front door has been carelessly left open, allowing harsh sounds of thunder to enter. The gaping door gives small glimpses into the outside world and the heavy storm violently brewing outside. Chloe's father appears to be holding something under his coat between his left arm and torso. As he stands in the entryway to the home, he wipes his work boots on a rubber welcome mat to prevent tracking mud farther inside. Drops of rain blow through the doorway and pelt the back of his neck. He quickly realizes that he has left the door open behind him, and to alleviate extra rainfall from entering the home, he slams the door shut.

Immediately, she notices a vividly painted look of contentment across her father's face that stems from the mere sound of the heavy door closing. As he treks further into the room with a rushed pace, he takes a moment to hear the door thud but does not exhibit enough care to watch it properly latch.

Chloe's curiosity grows from observing her father's rushed body language.

Hastily crossing the room, her father suddenly grasps that he is dripping water onto the wooden floorboards and recognizes that he is still wearing his drenched coat. Pausing for a moment, he removes his jacket, revealing a small square box wrapped in blue dinosaur-covered paper and adorned with a blue-and-yellow curled ribbon bow.

Chloe distinguishes it as a birthday present for her younger brother, Timothy.

Still, in a hurry, he throws the wet raincoat onto the floor and resumes walking. Looking across the room, He spots his wife across the room sitting on the ground with her head pressed against the couch. He rushes towards her. "Did you guys have cake yet?" he asks.

Infuriated by her husband's late arrival, she blames his absence for the terror of her situation and decides to punish him by not answering. She continues to hide her head in between the two couch cushions, ignoring his aggressive energy.

"I got held up at work again. I swear, I tried to get here as fast as traffic allowed," he says, but hearing the same explanation that she has attended numerous times before causes her to continue ignoring him.

His wife's lack of sympathetic forgiveness triggers him to stomp his feet loudly to elicit her attention as he approaches the couch.

Still pretending not to hear him, she raises her hands above her head and, with her face still concealed within the cushions of the couch, unties her long blonde hair from the unkempt updo on top of her head.

"You know how it is," he says softly while her face remains buried.

As she lightly moves her head from side to side, allowing her long dirty-blonde hair to tumble down her back. He takes another step towards her, still attempting to attain forgiveness. Now in closer proximity to his wife, he concludes she is face down on the couch, hiding her eyes, due to playing a game of hide-and-seek with the children.

Blatantly ignoring her husband, she digs her bony hands into her scalp to tease her hair. She creates friction with her fingers and releases an unnatural cackle that startles him. "Alright, children!" she says as she looks up at the white wall in front of her.

Her lack of attention toward him because of a game is not an acceptable excuse. He thinks he can sway her attention while she has her back to him, so he creeps closer to surprise her.

"I will give you until the count of ten before I come and get you!" she shouts. Remaining fixated on the wall, she counts down from the number ten. With a noticeable slur in her speech, her voice stumbles, causing the traditional number pattern to skip several digits in the progression.

Set on his plan to sneak up on his unsuspecting wife, he flirtatiously tickles her ribs and smirks. "Maybe you should just forget the seeking part," he says with a coy grin.

As he chuckles to get her to join in on the fun, her lack of reciprocation throws him off. Trying again to tickle her, she jumps from his fingers' touch and springs to her feet. His wife's skittish nature shocks him.

Focused on finishing the game's countdown, Chloe's mother lifts her right hand against her brow like a sailor looking for land. Turning around, she slowly climbs to her feet to scan the room, looking for the children.

The imbalanced rhythm of her shuffling steps leads her to stub her shin against the edge of the couch. The jolt to the sofa makes an empty bottle of whiskey fall to the floor from the edge of a cushion's crack and roll across the wood.

Chloe's father watches in disbelief as the glass bottle hits his grimy work boot. The sight of the stopped bottle evokes Chloe's father to seethe with anger. He reluctantly bends to the floor and, setting the present onto the ground, picks up the bottle with his hand. "Really?" he asks.

As he stands up, he reads the label on the bottle, clenching his jaw, and his face turns a shade of red.

"Ready or not...." the woman says. Continuing to ignore her scorching-mad husband, she tries to walk past him like he does not exist.

He tries to scare her by chucking the glass bottle at the wall behind her, barely missing her skull—shattered pieces of glass ricochet across the floor like rainfall. The harsh sound of the high-pitched echo causes Chloe to flinch and cover her ears.

Unfazed, her mother refuses to engage in her husband's childish ways and continues to walk away.

Irritated by his wife's lack of remorse, he aggressively grabs hold of her arm and yanks her closer. His pulling momentum shifts her hair, and it parts from her face, revealing a creepy grin.

Displeased by her condescending laughter, Chloe's father uses his opposite hand to retrieve one of the glass shards from the floor. "This is the shit you want to pull on our son's birthday?" he asks.

As he looks at the mess across the room's surfaces, his wife swats at his hand holding the piece of broken glass. Hitting his wrist, she knocks the shard out of his clutch.

"You're sick. You can't even put down the booze for an hour," he yells in her ear.

A smile takes over her mouth as she playfully makes clawing motions with her hands as if imitating a feral cat.

The sound of his wife hissing like a defensive feline provokes him to lose his temper. Releasing his wife's arm, he uses the free hand to hit her, and she falls to the ground.

Witnessing her father hitting her mom shocks Chloe, and placing her hand over her mouth, she silences her oncoming gasp.

Lying on the floor, her mother's breathing grows heavy, and she chuckles.

"What is wrong with you?!" he screams.

She lifts her head to mock him and feels a drop of blood roll down her chin from her busted lip. As she glares at him, she licks up the droplet of blood and grins.

"Oh, I know. You are just a fucking alcoholic," he states.

Looking at his wife with disgust, his eyes analyze her disheveled appearance, and he notices the deep cut on her leg. Her sharp fall to the floor causes the gash to hemorrhage more, and the sight makes him concerned for his children's safety.

"Where are the kids?" he asks with a tightened jaw. He lowers himself to the floor to match her eye level, forcing her to make eye contact with him.

Instead of answering, she hysterically laughs. As each snicker projects blood from her cut lip, she reaches into his back pocket and pulls out a red clown nose.

Angered by her uncaring personality, he leans closer and, watching her wince, sticks his finger deep into her wound. "Fucking answer me!" he shouts.

Spiteful from her husband's actions, she squeaks the red clown's nose and shrugs. "Maybe you should have become a clown! It probably would have paid better than your actual job," she says with a sneer. Grabbing his hand, she licks the blood from her wound off his fingers.

He snatches the clown's nose from her pinched fingers, seeing that she remains distracted. "You know, at least I'm taking care of my family... I put food on the table every night and this roof over our heads," he says.

His presentation of pointing at the ceiling makes her cackle with laughter. Raising his hand, he threatens to hit her again. "What the fuck did you do with them?" he shrieks.

The sight of him sweating with panic conjures a sinister smile to form across her lips. "I think I should ask the same of you. I hear you each night when you creep into her room with that same fucking song playing," she states, spitting with disgust.

Ignoring her accusation, he deflects, continuing to demand an answer by raising his voice. "What did you do with them, you drunken bitch?!" he yells.

Still maintaining eye contact as spit flies from his over enunciation, she dramatically shifts her eye line towards the dining-room door and shrugs her shoulders. "Timmy said he wanted cake," she states with a slur. Watching her husband's worried reaction makes her feel in control of the situation.

Jumping to his feet, he darts to the dining room to look for the children. Unable to locate either child, he returns to the living room and finds himself met with the image of his relaxed wife lying on the floor, awaiting his return. As she smirks, she points to the living room vent. "Ask that little cunt. I'm sure she's hiding your son from you," she states.

Chloe flinches as she inadvertently makes eye contact with her mother's wrathful glare.

Following the direction of his wife's pointing finger, her father turns to look and attaches the clown nose onto his face. He grins at the sight of Chloe's panicked eyes and waves his fingers.

Trying harder to stop herself from screaming, she covers her mouth even tighter with her hand. As she hears the record player turn on and play the familiar song, her psyche fills with terror. "No... no... no... no..." she mutters into her hand as a single teardrop falls from her eye.

The sound of heavy footsteps running from the living room prompts her to clutch the knife to her chest for protection. She hears a noise echo from the kitchen vent, and glancing back to look, she spots her dad prying open the grating and poking his head inside. "Come out, come out, wherever you are," he sings in a cheerful tone.

The sight of him startles her, and she scoots backward to escape.

"I'm not trying to hurt you," he says.

In an attempt to flee her dreaded father, she inches backward, deeper into the vent.

"I know that the cut on your mother's leg was an accident. We both can agree; she can be a bitch," he says with a cackle that echoes through the tin chamber.

Refusing to linger by listening for another moment longer, she twists her body to face the opposite direction and begins crawling rapidly.

Suddenly, she hears something behind her and, turning around, spots the Living Room Monster peering through the living room's vent opening. "Ready or not, here I come!" the creature shrills.

Using its spindle-like teeth, it tears the metal bars from their frame. The force of the act causes sparks to fly and land near Chloe's feet.

"When I get my hands on you, I won't be as forgiving," it says while making a chirping sound like a bird being eaten alive.

Terrified by the monster, she picks up her pace, crawling deeper into the lonely darkness. After traveling some distance, she feels she has finally reached a safe point and slows down her speed to catch her breath. Before she can take a single gulp of air, she hears what sounds like something crawling through the ducts from the direction of the kitchen.

"You've got to be brave for Timothy," she states. Her brother's disappearance fuels her mission, convincing her tired legs to keep going.

Observing a drastic drop in the temperature, she immediately notices that the hum of the air conditioning has been replaced with sounds of loud rustling swiftly heading toward her. Unexpectedly, she senses something seize her ankle, making it difficult to move.

Rather than fighting the resistance that holds her back, her body freezes. Slowly turning her head to identify the problem, her frustration turns to fear as she discovers that the force gripping her right ankle is the jagged fingernails of the Basement Monster.

"Slow down, child," the Basement Monster calls out with a snarl.

Panicked, she tries to free herself by fluttering her limb with all her might. With each kick of the leg that the Basement Monster clutches, she releases a tiny grunt, and her effort precipitates it to shake with laughter. "Where do you think you are going?" the creature asks with a giggle.

Watching the child's struggle causes the monster to fixate on her meaty foot and lick its lips. "If you run away from me, you will just make me sad," it says while dramatically howling. Loosely closing its lids over its eye sockets, it frowns.

Peeking through a single-eye crater, then two, it watches her reveling in her desperation. Entertained by her hand swinging the knife in its direction, it reaches out a creeping hand and pretends to touch the blade.

"Get back. I'm not afraid of you!" she shouts.

Giggling with excitement, the creature continues to feed off the little girl's fear and, using its spare hand, pounds the surrounding metal walls of the vent to simulate applause for her performance. "Oh, boy, do I have a fun idea!" it shouts with unbridled glee.

Sticking out its tongue in a flipping motion encourages saliva to spew from its mouth and drip to the vent ducts floor. "What if I rip that pretty tongue right from that tiny little mouth of yours?" the monster says.

The sight of Chloe's squirming foot becomes too enticing for the creature to resist. Reaching down to her flailing limb, it pulls her right shoe off and, holding it up to its discolored clown nose, deeply sucks in the aroma before swallowing the shoe in a single gulp.

Satisfied by the sour taste, it continues speaking to finish its thought. "Then would you be afraid, baby girl?" the creature asks.

Waiting for a response takes a moment of silence and gleans validation of her level of terror from her nervous mannerisms.

Shaking her head, she tries to avoid eye contact with the creature and closes her eyes, pretending to be brave.

Displeased by her response, which lacked rebutting substance, the monster tightens its grip around her foot for punishment. Hearing her ankle pop from the pressure, it snatches the opposite foot up in its hand.

Detaching its foot seizing arm from its socket, it single-handedly crawls up the side of the shallow tin wall and onto the vent's ceiling. Looking upside-down at Chloe, it inches closer to her face. "Oh, no?" it asks.

As she squirms to get away, she tries to keep her eyes closed. "No! I said I'm not afraid of you!" she screams.

Mere inches away from her face, it blows warm air into her eyes, giggling at her blatant lies. "Wrong answer, child," it says while maintaining an expressionless face.

Hearing a pause of silence fills her mind with anguish, making it impossible for her to grasp what is transpiring in the confined space entirely. Her eyes dart wide open to see what is happening around her. Met by the sight of the clowns clanking teeth heckling her shaking leg, she releases an ear-piercing scream.

Slowly elongating its digits, the creature reaches into her gaping mouth to pinch her dancing tongue. As it fights the squirming tongue between its two fingers, it slowly drags it out of her mouth. "Cat got your tongue?" the monster playfully asks.

The image of the child's tongue stretching puts a grin on his face as its texture mimics a taffy-like consistency one could find at a carnival. "Maybe next time, you'll think twice before you squeal like a little piglet," it says with a laugh while holding her detached tongue between its fingers.

Chloe tries to speak, but with her obstructed voice, nothing is clear.

Drooling with built-up saliva, the creature devours her tongue like a fruit roll-up. As she looks cross-eyed at her disappearing appendage, her eyes water from the unbearable pain, and she panics.

"My, my, you sure are delicious," it says in a garbled tone as its esophagus fills to the brim with the lengthy organ. Continuing to slurp, the Basement Monster comes nose to nose with Chloe and gives her a toothy grin.

Eyeing the last piece of the tongue rooted to the bottom of her mouth causes the creature to drool with desire. With the point of its finger, it forcefully reaches between her teeth and harpoons her tongue like skewered meat. The jagged nail impaling her nerve-filled flesh triggers jolting pain to surge through her body. Her wincing prompts the knife to drop from her hand.

Pure ecstasy invades every limb of the Basement Monster as it tears the final piece from her mouth. It watches the small child cover her lips with her hands as he slurps the rest of her severed tongue into his throat. The act of her clutching her face with her unsteady hands shows the creature the true extent of her excruciating pain.

"You look frightened, little girl," it whispers. Creeping down from the vent's ceiling, it backs into the shadows far enough to continue watching the show of agony in peace.

As Chloe's mouth fills with blood, it overflows its capacity and begins dripping from the corners of her lips. She is terrified to see the creature's glowing eyes shift wildly in circles of excitement.

Its arm stretches toward her, and, using its elongated finger, it scoops up the bodily fluid from her face and uses the crimson liquid to paint a board game-sized hopscotch pattern on the tin floor. Its spidery fingers mimic legs skipping towards the child's feet and tap within the parameters of the blood-painted course.

"Now that I've had a delicious snack, what do you say we play an actual game?" it whispers with a snarl. Bored by the one-sided game of hopscotch, it acts like a cat playing with a mouse and slides across the vent, batting its bony fingers through the air at her feet.

She feels helpless as she watches the terrifying being that ate her tongue approach her. As she scoots backward to get away, the Basement Monster springs out of the shadows and grabs her left ankle and her remaining shoe. Using its spindly fingers, it drags her closer.

Unable to stop her momentum, she clutches her mouth tighter to seal off her pain and begins choking on the hemorrhaging blood. Her mouth jolts open as she frantically gasps for air, causing a waterfall of gore to stream down her chin.

She trembles as the creature removes the remaining shoe from her foot and stretches out its arm to nonchalantly dip the shoe in the fresh pool of blood, then eats it.

"Here are the rules," it states. Scratching its chin to think of what is next, it lifts a finger into the air to signal that the rules of the game are ready to be heard. "If you scream..." it says while smirking. Unable to control its giggles, it removes the dirty, frilly sock from her left foot and wiggles each of her toes.

Blood loss causes Chloe's energy to dwindle and her mind to drift on the edge of consciousness. She does not have the strength required to respond to his playful tickles.

"...I will happily pet these little piggies," it states. Finishing its sentence, it slinks closer to her barefoot and raises it to its face for a long sniff. As it licks the drool from its lips, it lets out a loud squeal of excitement.

"If you can't..." the creature says.

Excited to regurgitate the details of the child's horrible fate, the Basement Monster releases a cackle, showing its grotesque jagged teeth. "...I will eat each one whole," it states with a sadistic grin.

Chloe's eyes widen with terror. Gathering enough adrenaline, her body spirals into fight-or-flight mode to survive. Quietly patting the darkness beside her, she is met by a sharp poke from the tip of the cold metal blade and winces. As she watches the Basement Monster move its mouth closer to her barefoot, she keeps her focus locked on its whereabouts and, shifting her grip, grabs the knife's handle.

Infatuated by the child's soft skin, the creature wiggles her big toe with its pointed fingernail. Seeing it distracted, she seizes her opportunity and hides the knife behind her back.

"You ready to play?" the Basement Monster says with glee.

Reluctant to answer the creature, she remains silent, hoping it will go away and she will return to her warm bed. Even though she knew the abuse that waited in her bedroom, she felt that at that moment, anything would be better than her current hellish predicament.

More expansive than before, the creature opens its mouth. As it makes eye contact with the panicked child, it places her entire wiggling foot in the gaping orifice. "I just want a tiny taste to tide me over...," the Basement Monster says. Initially contented by a few licks, the creature releases the foot from its mouth and takes a moment to inhale her fear.

Chloe closes her eyes and attempts to gain the courage to fight. She has her life to defend and her brother's as well.

"I'm not afraid of you!" she yells tongueless, blood-spewing with each word spoken.

The child's disrespect incites the Basement Monster's demeanor to shift from playfulness to pure evil, and it determinedly lifts her foot to its quivering lips.

As its mouth reopens to take the first bite of her delicate flesh, she closes her eyes in anticipation of the torture. Wildly stabbing the knife before her, she attempts to postpone the inevitable amputation.

With her last bit of breath, she releases a bloodcurdling scream from her gurgling throat, and the music playing in the living room stops.

Chapter Nine

BUBBLE BATHS

Though something feels different to Chloe, she refuses to open her eyes and face the reality of her new situation. Instead, she takes a moment of silence to listen for any noticeable differences. As she absorbs the room's ambiance through her patient eardrums, her mind becomes disoriented. The relaxing sound of trickling water has replaced the ominous sound of the record player.

Wafting smells of cheap soap cause her mind to refocus on subsequent sensory triggered memories. The familiar scent trapped in the humidity reminds her of the cherished warm bubble baths she used to take. Treated as a form of reward, her parents would allow her one each month if she performed a behavior deemed worthy of praise. Carried away within the daydream created by the smells of positive reinforcement, she loses track of time.

The sound of trickling water immediately reminds her that she must use the bathroom and her legs tightly cross to combat the aching sensation. Her full bladder brings about flashbacks of wetting herself in front of her classmates, and as she relives the humiliation of the incident, her optimistic vision of bubble baths is ripped from her mind. She quickly recalls her mother's arrival when picking her up from school, and her stale attitude made it clear that her bath privileges for the month would be revoked.

Knowing for sure that the sound of the running bath water is not for her prompts a stomachache brought on by her anxiety. Ignoring the warning signs from her gut, she changes her emotional trajectory by taking a deep breath. Meditatively, she slowly sifts the humid room's air in through her nostrils and out through her mouth, calming her.

The sound of the bathwater running makes her imagination take flight toward positive ruminations. Fantasizing about the porcelain tub filling with steaming bubbly water creates a happy euphoria in her mind. She remembers that watching the bath fill with her monthly prize always helps her shaking body calm down. Gradually, she cracks her eyes open and is met with rejuvenation.

Wiggling her toes, she assesses whether the Basement Monster followed through with amputating her foot with its teeth. Her movement is met with a sensation that tingles in her tendons, making her realize that her extremities are still intact. Looking down at her bare feet, she feels her fear lifted from her rib cage, and she can breathe again.

As she takes a moment to unwind, the fact that the Basement Monster can no longer terrorize her sinks in, and her body sighs. To her, peace resembles the contentment created by the smell of a foaming bubble bath. Sensing an unfamiliar movement in her lips, she relaxes her facial muscles. She lets them twist into a grin as she allows herself to accept that the warm scent, combined with her being safe, has created an unusual state of happiness inside of her core.

Taking an additional second to cherish the jubilant feelings that she has been praying for, she continues to bask in the accomplishment of her escape. As she senses adequacy, she refocuses her attention on her feet. Scanning herself from her feet to her legs, she realizes she is standing on a stool in front of the bathroom sink. The familiarity of the surrounding scenery is part of her usual nighttime routine and makes perfect sense to her.

She does not recall sleepwalking, but her current placement makes her believe she must have had a nightmarish dream. Condemned in the past for walking in her sleep by her mother, she concludes that she is correct and that this whole monstrous ordeal could be another episode. The thought of being able to chalk up the day's series of events to a long bout of somnambulism further calms her.

Immediately, she wishes to get back to her routine. Shifting her gaze away from the stool, she looks at the fogged vanity mirror in front of her. As the room temperature rises, she observes the growing condensation on the glass, and something above the mirror catches her attention.

Investigating directly above the obscured reflection, her eyes become preoccupied with the vanity's flickering lightbulbs. Her optimism about the previous events, only being horrible dreams, quickly shatters as the sound of the downstairs record player begins to play. Trying to listen closer, she can hear the familiar nightmarish song accent the consistent white noise from the bathtub faucet.

The eerie melody causes her underlying panic to return and her fist to tighten. With her hand still clutching onto a handle, she is provided the confidence to fight back. As she finds stability within her gripping fingers, her eyes look down towards her hand to admire the weapon, and she is startled by her findings. Her trusted butcher knife has been replaced by the same pink toothbrush she uses every day for her morning and nighttime routine.

Defeated by the fact that she has been left without a means of protection, she is distraught. "Make it stop," she cries.

Her hands tremble by her sides. Shaking with fear, her welling eyes give in to her building hysterics, and she drops the toothbrush to the floor. She tries to gather her emotions and comfort herself by using her pajama's oversized sleeve to wipe her eyes. "Why is this happening to me?" she says with a sniffle.

As she gasps for help, her body buckles beneath her from the emotional trauma. Following in order, her hands start to shake, then her torso, and then her knees knock together. "Please, can someone help me?" she whimpers.

The sight of the unresponsive white popcorn-textured ceiling deepens her dismay as she looks up and desperately tries to communicate to any higher power that will lend a caring ear. Between each plea, she pauses, hoping that someone above will hear her cries for help, sure that if only a divine presence would see the volatility of her situation, it might save her from the misery.

"I give up," she sobs. Shrugging, she signals her defeat like a soldier waving a flag of surrender.

While her stare is locked dead on the textured bumps of the ceiling, she discovers a patch of discolored spackle that intrigues her. Looking closer into the obscurity of the grotesque coloring, she tries to sharpen her vision by squinting.

The steaming mist has caused water damage to the textured grooves, and each uniquely discolored piece of mildewy wallpaper resembles pulsing veins embellished by sprouting green mold buds. The putrid floral pattern swiftly grows as the hot bath water runs.

"Please, please, please—someone, please help," she pleads.

As she keeps her head tilted up to the ceiling, the water from her tears creates pool formations in her eye sockets. Refusing to let them drain, she tries to deny her sorrow the right to flourish.

Eventually, unable to retain another drop, she closes her eyes to protect her pupils from the salty fluid, releasing the pent-up tears. Slowing the pace of her breathing, she tries to calm her nerves. The puffing air from each exhalation expels the thick snot from her nose horizontally across her cheeks.

"If not me, please just help Timothy," she cries.

Hearing no response between her sniffles, she continues to fall deeper into her escalating depression. Overtaken by desperation, her eyes frantically shift away from the water-damaged ceiling to her indistinct reflection in the mirror. Fixated on the blurred image that looks back at her from the vanity, she attempts to find her pupils. "Whoever is doing this to me needs to listen!" she screams.

Leaning closer to the skewed image, she notices that her fogged mirror reflects a muddled pinkish tone caused by her screaming, turning her face a dark shade of red. The hue resembles her mother's after finishing one of her daily belittling tirades.

Terrified by the likeness, Chloe takes a couple of deep breaths to calm herself down before continuing her plea for help. "I promise to be good," she says.

Believing that she has run out of options to get someone's attention for help, she reaches for the material of the pajamas. Straightening up her appearance, she makes herself look less chaotic. "I don't want to play games anymore. I want my brother back," she says.

As she finishes untwisting her nightclothes, her hands grab the pink fabric that makes up the collar around her neck. She dabs her fallen tears and cleans the dirt smudges from her face using the material.

As she neurotically scrubs the accumulated filth from her cheeks, she remembers her failed attempt at escaping through the ventilation system and sniffling to stop her tears, her jaw clenches.

Wanting a better view of her face, she stands on her tiptoes to get a more detailed look in the vanity mirror. She winces at the feeling of her flexing calve muscles straining and ignores each ache so that she can assure her face is cleaned to her father's liking. Worried that the image she is using may be too blurry to see the dirt's placement accurately, she lifts her palm to clear it and uses her petite hand to defog the mirror, unveiling a clearer picture of the bathtub behind her.

As she brushes away the mirror's condensation, she gets a better look at her reflection and gruesomely reveals a putrid arm dangling from the side of the porcelain tub. Caught off guard by the repulsive visual behind her, she causes her hands wiping motion to come to a halt. Her pupils enlarge into a state of shock. Not wanting to turn around, she leans closer and fixes her stare on the horrific image she has uncovered in the mirror's reflection.

Convincing herself that her imagination plays tricks on her makes her feel more at ease. Her shaking hand stabilizes on the glass, and she continues slowly moving her hand to wipe the remaining fog away. Terrified by the image still present in the mirror, she looks away as she cleans and places her second hand on top of the first to calm the harsh tremors.

As she attempts to avoid looking at the image firsthand, she stands higher on her toes to investigate it through the vanity at a different angle to get a better look. Analyzing the scene triggers terror to flow through her blood.

The body attached to the mangled hand is her father. His floating body is bloated from the effects of decomposition and extreme fluid retention caused by inhaling water into his lungs. The distended stomach of his corpse has broken the buttons off his ill-fitted black suit. Each coattail has picked a side of his body, and they wade in the water next to him with his small floating derby hat. On his feet are his old worn-out scuffed work boots.

She is unable to break her curious gaze. Looking closer into the beveled glass, she uses the mirror as a shielding wall of protection from the gruesome scene. Analyzing the parameters of the tub, she pays close attention to see if she can recognize any of the articles of clothing her father is wearing. Immediately, as her line of sight moves to eye his work boots, the color of the steaming water and soapy bubbles catches her attention. The murky suds are an unusual shade of rose-petal pink and do not match her memory associated with the smell.

Trying to comprehend the odd tinge of color, her traveling eyes scan his body. As she makes it halfway up his left thigh, her eyes skittishly jump to look at the floating derby hat. The pattern of the rippling waves caused by the water pouring from the faucet taps the soaked felt hat against the corpse's hip, and the hypnotizing movement causes her to fall into a trance. She feels like the world is spinning in a psychedelic circle.

Chloe watches the corpse's buoyant fingertip lift, bumping the brim of the hat and the subtle jostling allows a red ball to drift from underneath its felt hiding place. The clown nose bobs like a slithering snake through the water's building wake performing a relaxed dance. With every dodge of each small ripple, her eyes follow the ball's treacherous path downstream. The floating object travels to a section of the tub's water that is more condensed with color and comes to an abrupt stop. Gradually camouflaged by the murky liquid, the round ball disintegrates into the depths of the porcelain tub.

Confused by the ball's whereabouts, her vision broadens to look for it, and her wandering eye lands upon the mutilated neck of the corpse. The exact string missing from the bobbing clown's nose is wrapped tightly around his neck.

Gasping at the bloody sight, she squints to make the image clearer through her watering eyes and sees that the strangling material has cut through each layer of flesh. The taut elasticity of the line makes the task of slicing through skin look effortless. The sight makes Chloe form her final hypothesis that the seeping wound is the reason for the rosy water, and her stomach becomes queasy over the gruesome revelation.

As she closes her eyes to take a break from the morbid sight, her mind continues to permanently etch the image of the nearly decapitated body onto the backside of her eyelids.

Frantically trying to reset her tainted mind, she taps the side of her head to create a blank-thinking state.

Her effort lacking success makes her upset stomach dry heave. Curling her torso over the edge of the sink, she tries to rid herself of her festering sickness by throwing up. Jolting sideways from a mighty heave causes her limbs to lose balance, and the stool slides out from underneath her; as a splashing sound accompanies her fall to the floor, panic swirls through her thoughts.

Picking up her hands from the overflowing tub of water, she quickly notices that the watered-down blood has stained them light red. Still holding her hands in front of her face, she watches as they begin to tremble. Instead of looking at the gruesome scene from afar, she is now amid the chaos. Turning her body to face the tub, she directly observes the corpse, rather than relying on the mirror's secondhand account, making the clarity of the image much crisper.

As she takes in the details of the traumatic sight, her mind takes a long pause to process the scene. Starting at the nape of the neck, her eyes slowly work their way up to her father's face, where she is met by a buildup of green decay combined with matted clown makeup. The oxidized makeup on his lips partially covers the tone of dark purple in his skin from oxygen deprivation and putrefaction. His bottom jaw has been unaligned from the top, and his pale tongue hangs, partially impaled by his teeth.

Becoming deeply sickened by the image, she tries to look away, and her eyes catch a glimpse of her father's nose, causing a rush of horror to sweep over her mind.

A mutilated hole sits where the corpse's nose should be. The skin that surrounds the severed facial feature has been painted burgundy red. Pulsing tinges of gangrenous puss ooze down the sides of his teeth. Afraid to lose her nose, her hands fling up from the water to cup her face.

As her hand bursts from the shallow liquid, a butcher knife falls from her grip and lands with a splash. Not remembering the knife still in her grasp, her eyes widen with terror as she frantically scurries to get away from the weapon.

She frenziedly scoots backward across the water-covered floor to escape, pricking her toe on something sharp as she kicks. Chloe's eyes remain locked on the knife, and her movement abruptly terminates when her back forcefully hits the wall behind her. Running her hand back and forth across the obstruction, she nervously picks at the white textured wallpaper peeling from the condensation and attempts to reaffirm her surroundings.

Using each trembling fingertip to peer behind the section of fallen wallpaper, her eyes become paralyzed by what's underneath. Stuffed behind the damp boards are heaps of dried autumn leaves. Retracting her hands back to her sides, she stares at the wall with building remorse as she is brought back to the memory of playing in the leaves.

Reflecting on the countless nights that she prayed for God to remove her father from her life, she assumes her selfishness is to blame for his demise. The guilt drives her soul deeper into a depressive state. "Daddy," she whispers.

Afraid to acknowledge the inevitable silence, she does not want to confirm her greatest fear and accept emotional guilt for his death. Sitting silently in the stagnant air, her body is overtaken by a flurry of emotions, and she starts to bawl hysterically. "I didn't mean to tell anyone," she whimpers.

Hoping that the sound of her voice will wake him from his deep slumber like a children's tale, she continues to force herself to talk to him, mentally convincing herself that the reason for his lack of speech is her words being unpersuasive.

"You can touch me if that makes this stop. I promise I will be good," Chloe mumbles over the sound of the running bathwater.

So that he can better hear her speech, she gets on all fours to get closer. As she crawls nearer to the horrifying scene, her trembling hands inadvertently splash water droplets tasting of iron into her gasping mouth. Reaching the base of the porcelain tub, she covers her mouth to stop herself from screaming, and warm tears drip down her hands.

Her emotional state shifts from horrific shock to sadness as she mourns the loss of her parent. Processing that the only father figure she has ever known is deceased creates a heavy sorrow in her heart. She removes her trembling hands from her mouth and stretches her fingers to comfort his limp hand. "I didn't mean it, Daddy! You're not old. You are my favorite," she cries.

Continuing to sob, she begs for forgiveness. As she rubs each of his fingertips, she desperately searches for any possibility of hidden warmth and rests her head on his lifeless arm. "I will be different," she says as her tears tumble toward his decaying corpse.

Realizing that there is nothing she can do to bring him back, she spirals into a panic. Suffocating anxiety smothers her as she thinks about how her mother will react to the news. With her head in her hands, she covers her eyes and curls her body into a ball while rocking herself back and forth to calm her nerves.

Nearly at the point of taming her angst, she feels her focus ripped away by loud knocking sounds. The sound sends vibrations through the still water, causing Chloe to jump. The music on the record player stops, and, for a moment, she is a bit more at ease.

"Open the door, baby. I know that you're in there," her mother says.

The sound of her mother's voice makes Chloe's swirling thoughts resume and, to mute them, she rocks her body at a faster pace. Remaining silent, she waits for her mother to leave her alone.

"I know what you did..." her mother says.

Loudly pounding her fists to get her daughter's attention, her soft voice is contradicted. "Just let me in so that I can help you figure this out," she says.

The tone of her voice is different from anything Chloe has heard from her before; it is inviting. Growing confused by her mother's unsolidified personality, she feels overwhelmed by the situation unfolding. In response to the instability, she clutches her hair for comfort as she curls into a tighter fetal position for safety. "I didn't do anything. I didn't hurt anyone," she cries.

Rocking her body at a faster pace, tears stream down her cheeks as she looks into the open eyes of her deceased father. "I just want this to stop," Chloe sobs.

Knocking louder on the wooden door, her mother interrupts her building lamentation. "It's not yours or anyone's fault, sweetie," she says.

Still swept up in her frazzled thoughts, Chloe imagines the sounds of each knock falling into a rhythmic pattern like a beating heart. Covering her ears, she tries to stop the harsh tones from haunting her.

"We can't help the cards we're dealt, but I promise I can make it better if you just let me in," she says.

The comforting tone kindles a false sense of hope to engulf Chloe's mind. Thinking that for the first time in her life, her mother may want to help her compels Chloe to look in the door's direction to listen.

"We can get through this together," her mother states.

As she takes a last look at her father, Chloe feels the emotional weight of all the traumatic experiences she has encountered in her lifetime thrust upon her shoulders. "If I open the door, I swear, I will be good, momma," she says. Her voice wavers as she weighs out her potential options for escape.

Delicately knocking, her mother uses the back of her hand to let her daughter know that she has not abandoned her. "All you have to do is let me in," she says.

Inching closer to her father's face, Chloe stands over him to say goodbye. She reaches behind his bobbing head to turn off the running faucet and takes a deep breath in the dead silence.

Unable to unlock her gaze, she notices that his bulging eyes and rough skin sit on his face like an unrecognizable leatherlike mask, and the sight causes Chloe to be torn by mixed emotions. Wiping her nose, she continues to look at his floating body as she moves toward the wall next to the bathroom door.

Her back resting against the unyielding wood allows her to stabilize her weak stance. She can feel her beating heart normalizing as she clutches her chest and places her hand on the door handle without taking a moment to think. Slowly turning the knob, the overflowing water pours into the hallway as she cracks the door.

"I'm ready to listen, momma," Chloe timidly says through the crack.

Raising her ear to the slit, she listens for the sound of her mother's footsteps coming to rescue her like a knight in shining armor. The consistent silence causes Chloe to feel defeated.

She pushes the bathroom exit the rest of the way open, searching for her mother. As she peers outside, she is flooded with confusion. There is no sign of her. Still compelled by the reassuring statements that had given her hope for survival, her feet venture further into the hallway to search for her. "Momma?" she calls out to the dark abyss.

Finding herself completely alone, she hears the distant needle from the record player scratch. Shivers run down her spine as she recognizes the triggering familiar song starting to play.

"I promise, I will be good and listen," she says. Met with no response, she is frozen with fear.

Chapter Ten

NO BOYS ALLOWED

Without a single sign from her mother, her feet refuse to move, leaving her waiting alone in the darkness, and despair overtakes her.

The lack of lighting in the hallway triggers her mind to hyper-focus on thoughts involving the predicament of her loneliness. Believing that another parental figure has abandoned her makes her feel submissive and want nothing more than to give up fighting for her mediocre life. If there is truth in her mother's prior suggestions, maybe she should give up on her meaningless existence.

Her promise to her brother and the fact that her mother may be the sole successor for his care are the only things giving her the will to continue.

Made furious by her immobile legs, her heart attempts to send a convincing reason to her fossilized feet so they will transport her. The internal conflict causing her static motion provokes her mind, triggering it to replay old memories like a projector.

Each of the reminiscences unfolding behind the corneas of her eyes encompasses the moments she had consistently made promises to her younger brother. "No matter what, we have each other," she says. The thought of them being together eased her deepest fears of abandonment.

As Chloe's head finishes with her memories reiterations, she is sure of one thing: if she ever wants to experience the presence of her brother again, she must persevere. Pumping her hands repeatedly into fists, she forces her blood to flow into her arms, which are falling asleep. It thrills her to feel the prickling tingles of each waking finger, prompting her arms to wiggle like jelly. The small sign of movement allows her body to sway. Building the momentum to travel to her toes, all she wants is to make her legs move, to take one step of any size forward.

Using her sense of purpose to create a plan of action to find her brother, her eyes cautiously scan the dark hallway. At the opposite end of the long corridor, her gaze is drawn to an unfamiliar stained-glass window. The positioning of the casement sitting near Timothy's room makes her emotionally restless.

Perturbed that she cannot place the beautiful piece of artwork within her memory, she wonders if her whole recollection of everything prior had been incorrect. The notion that she only remembers the traumatizing visions continuously haunting her soul is unsettling. In all her time living within the house's cold partitioning walls, she had never noticed the beauty of the window she had sauntered by every day and night. Making up for a lost time, she takes a moment to revel in the beauty of the deeply toned arched window that now calls to her.

The installation of Gothic art is constructed of tiny shards of colored glass. Accented by the dark tones of the night sky, each different section portrays a slightly gloomy stylistic touch. As the moon casts slivering tinges of yellow light through the fused framework, it projects a formation onto the floor. The silhouette produced on the ground in front of her depicts an archangel that is upside down.

Intrigued by the placement of the image with religious tones, Chloe's mind wonders if it has been placed there as a sign.

Growing up with two parents practicing different denominations, she remembers vicious fights and slamming doors like clockwork every Sunday morning. Her parents could never concur on whose ideological view would comprise the foundation they would instill in their children.

Instead of agreeing, they argued that the other acted holier than thou. In the end, both spitefully declared atheism and spewed loathing words at the religion each had been raised to devoutly practice. On the same day of the declaration regarding the household's non-religious view, the couple hatefully burned any relic that symbolized the other's religious affiliation. Nothing considered holding a spiritual connection was allowed within the home's four walls from that moment forward.

Never seeing a single object inside the household tied to religious principles leads Chloe to feel a deep urge in her gut that the extended portrait has been put in her path to relay an important message. As she cautiously makes her way towards the faith-provoking artwork, her ears open, honing in on each intricately detailed noise. At first, seeming to be met only by harsh tranquility, the sudden sound of a woman's cry causes her body to stiffen.

She takes a moment to cease her movement and silently listens for the source of the mournful howl as she hears the reverberation of the second wail coming from the direction of the angelic formation, her finicky nerves instantly calm. Before taking another step forward, her body leans to get a better look at whatever creature may be causing the disturbing noise.

Trying to focus her vision away from the projection of moonlight under the base of the stained-glass window, she makes out the faint outline of a huddling figure. Entrenched in the investigation of the distant form, she becomes complacent about her surroundings, and the sudden sound of the bathroom door slamming shut causes her to jump. Driven by fear, she quickly reacts to the noise and cocks her head behind her to look.

"Timothy... is that you?" she asks.

Met with pure silence, her energy refocuses on observing the mysterious figure in the distance. Taking a deep inhalation of courageous breath, her legs continue to walk toward the ornate window. As she watches the expanse between her and the end of the hallway close in, the image of the crying woman becomes unmistakable, and she realizes the familiar face belongs to her mother. Picking up her pace, she worries that the root of her mother's tears has been caused by not finding her. Chloe runs toward her to provide comfort.

Only a foot away, she observes her mother's stooped body in the hallway's corner, dressed in an outfit indicative of her sadness. She is wearing a plain black modest dress with low black matching heels, and her hair is pinned away from her face with a nondescript metal clip. Her mother's strictly black attire combined with the tone of her sobbing verifies that the loss of a loved one fuels her mournful cries.

Making sure no monsters are around to hurt them, she looks to both ends of the hallway and verifies they are safe, then approaches to console her mother. "Are you okay, momma?" she quietly asks.

Loudly weeping and consumed by her misery, her mother does not hear her small daughter, causing her to ignore the question.

"What's wrong?" Chloe asks.

As she listens to each of her mother's pleading cries, Chloe's body begins to embody her mother's excruciating pain. Thinking her words have triggered a reaction, she watches her mother slowly lift her head from her hands. With a full view of her hidden face, Chloe can see the true extent of her despair.

Her mascara runs from her swollen eyelids as she looks past her daughter towards the closed bathroom door. She does not acknowledge her, causing Chloe to feel invisible. Waving her hands, she attempts to get her mother's attention.

Desperate to experience human touch, she reaches her tiny hand towards her mother. "I'm right here, momma," she says.

As Chloe is about to tap her shoulder, she springs to her feet and takes a step past her, dodging the comforting touch.

Trying to get her attention, Chloe turns her body to face her mother's back. "It's me, Chloe," she says.

Giving no sign of acknowledgment to her daughter, her mother continues her path towards the bathroom door. The act of her mother pretending like she does not exist makes Chloe feel forsaken. Her eyes tear up more with each step she watches her mother take.

"Please just look at me," she pleads, failing to grab her attention, as her mother still deliriously paces down the hallway. Without taking a moment to look back, she releases a heavy sigh as she places her hand on the bathroom doorknob and lets herself in. Shutting the door behind her prompts a sickening scream to exit her body as she joins her husband. Chloe is left alone.

"You can't leave. I need you," Chloe says with despair.

Wanting to recapture a taste of the love that her mother brandished through the bathroom door, Chloe's body picks up speed, running after her, desperate to relive the compassion she had experienced through the woman's fibbing words. As she reaches the shut door, her trembling hand probes for the dented doorknob.

"You can do this. Just breathe," she says. Listening to her own words of encouragement, she closes her eyes to recenter herself and focuses on trying to calm the jittery sensation prickling down her spine. "It's just a bathroom," she states.

She reminds herself that nothing is usually as wrong as it seems, and her shakiness dissipates. Opening her eyes, her stare is met by the wooden door that stands protecting her. "You wouldn't have made it this far if you weren't a big girl, so no turning back. You have to find Timothy," she states confidently.

Upon the exhalation of her final deep breath, she opens the door, and immediately, the bathroom lights turn off. Peering inside the darkroom from the hallway, her eyes begin to adjust, and she is bewildered by what she sees.

There is no sign of her dad's decaying body. It is gone, and the bathroom has been returned to a state of normalcy.

Still on her mission to find her mother, she takes a step closer and slowly pokes her head inside the doorway to get a better look. Glancing to the left, she is met with disappointment. She scans the room to the right, and an overwhelming smell of burning cake hits her.

Chloe steps inside the room to identify the source of the smell, and as her curious eyes peek around the back of the wood door, she finds herself face to face with the Living Room Monster. Its two black marble eyes spark the memory of the creature nearly devouring her skull, and she screams in terror.

As she rapidly tries to escape, her fumbling hands shove open the door, causing her to fall back into the hallway. Her overwhelming angst causes her knees to buckle, and she collapses to the floor.

The creature remains inside the bathroom. Witnessing it scaling up the wall backward, she can see its glowing eyes spin through the gaping doorway. She watches its head twist on a single vertebra as it crosses the threshold and transitions onto the hallway ceiling. "She is gone, just like everyone else in your life," the Living Room Monster says while snarling hatefully.

The sight of the monster approaching from above makes Chloe's body inch backward.

"She doesn't love you. She never has, and never will," the creature shrieks with a witch-like cackle.

Hearing the words upsets Chloe. Shaking her head in disagreement, she attempts to convince herself that the foul words are faulty. "That's not true!" she yells.

As the creature scales closer, her panicked throat releases a cry for help while she scurries backward to escape its grasp.

"She promised she's going to save me," Chloe shouts.

The sound of her words elicits the Living Room Monster to grin like a bird waiting for its mother to regurgitate food. It continues to crawl unnaturally, like a spider on the ceiling above the child's head, until it comes to a perching stop to watch her squirm.

The grotesque smile fills Chloe with terror as she watches the skin on each corner of its elongated mouth split. The monster's jaw loudly cracks as it dislocates and continues to extend like that of an anaconda preparing to engulf its prey.

Adrenaline jolts through Chloe's body, prompting her extremities to pick up the pace of her frantic backward crawl.

Swimming through the air like electric eels, the colorless hair of the creature extends from the ceiling to the floor. As each follicle takes on a life of its own, it disperses like sticky cobwebs trying to snare its prey. Chloe's scrambling feet propel her further towards the staircase.

"Let's play a game," the monster says.

Not wanting to partake in another sadistic ordeal, the child continues her retreat, using her hands to feel the texture of the floorboards behind her to guide her direction. "Where is my brother?" she says.

The monster demonically cackles at the child fighting back the tears as it enjoys the evolving spectacle. "In my belly," it squeals. Removing a single hand from the ceiling to pat its distended stomach, it mocks her sadness.

Apprehensive of breaking eye contact with the creature, her hands identify the edge of the top stair. Touching the steep dead-end confirms her anguish, and she knows she has nowhere to go. "I just want my brother!" Chloe cries.

Each tear streaming down the child's face creates a new hunger pain in the monster's stomach triggering its organs to release an unsettling growl.

"Give him back! I want him back," Chloe wails.

The Living Room Monster's howling laughter causes its head to swing like a momentous pendulum, and the violent sway causes its last vertebrae to snap. Flinching at the noise of its breaking neck, Chloe cowers to shield her face.

As she timidly peeks through her fingers, she can see the emancipated head beginning to advance towards her. Using its serpent-like tongue to gain traction against the floorboards, its head creeps closer with an undulating crawl, slowly making its way to the shaking child. Chloe stares in a catatonic state due to the image sparking gruesome memories of her father's nearly decapitated corpse.

Licking the ground surrounding her foot, the creature comes closer, and she snaps back to reality. "I can take you to him," the beast says with a childlike giggle that sounds identical to her brothers.

Chloe immediately recognizes that it is only an emotional manipulation. Wildly scanning for an escape, she inadvertently makes eye contact with the smirking head, and it instantly transforms into the head of her mother.

"You are not my mother!" Chloe says, fiercely kicking her feet at it to force it to stay away. Playing off the child's deepest desires, the scheming head begins to cry.

Seeing the child cannot look away from the sobbing face, the monster takes a moment to scale quietly down the wall. Reaching the floor, it picks up the head to coddle it. It rocks the head back and forth in its arms as the nose starts to sniffle, and as it places the mother's head on its neck, it wipes the dripping snot. Incorporating the human likeness stimulates the rest of the creature's body to shape-shift to match. As the transformation into her mother nears completion, the monster extends a single hand out to Chloe.

"See, baby, it's me," it says.

She was staring at what now looks like her mother confuses the child, causing her to question her reality.

"Just give me your hand, and we can make this all go away," it says. Extending its palm towards Chloe, it takes a step closer. Its hand opens wider and offers to help the little girl stand to her feet.

Overwhelmed with ambivalence, Chloe pulls away and cries. She scampers backward to the furthest point possible on the top step and sits in silence as she sorts through her vacillating thoughts.

"It's me; you can relax now," it states.

Focusing on the tone of her mother's voice, Chloe finds the same euphoric sensations of love she had felt in the bathroom, and her eyes widen. "Momma?" she says. Her understanding of what love should feel like engulfs her soul and stops her body from tremoring. "Is that you?" she asks.

Softly smiling, it nods to reassure Chloe and further extends its palm to offer help.

Desperately optimistic, Chloe stretches her frail arm and reaches for its welcoming grip. As their fingers touch, she swiftly retracts her hand. To her horror, she recognizes that one of the welcoming digits is tipped with the sharpened black nail of the Living Room Monster.

Uncertain as to why the child pulled away, it glances down at its digits, and upon seeing the divulging nail, it immediately tucks it away behind its back. "Come here,

Chloe, just come to momma," it says while masking its impatience.

She is convinced that the loathsome enemy has ripped away any hope of experiencing her mother's love, and the once empty void now overflows with despising rage.

"Let's get you to bed so you can get some sleep," it says in a demonic tone.

The child glares daggers at the thing standing before her, and her seething hatred turns her face red. "You are not my mother!" Chloe screams.

Jumping to her feet, her jaw clenches as she grits her teeth, and for the first time in her life, she believes herself invincible. "You are a monster!" she yells as she points at the creature.

Letting out the years of built-up hatred, she refuses to hold any of her feelings back. Chloe is finished with being a victim. "You are not my mother!" she cries. Stomping her feet to build traction against the wood, she charges at its legs.

Attempting to evade Chloe's rage-fueled charge, it sidesteps. Not anticipating the tremendous force of her impact, the monster is thrown off guard by the brutality of her tackle, and unable to stabilize its footing, it loses its balance. Its hands desperately flail, reaching for anything to hold on to stop its fall, but its slow reflexes cause the attempts to fail.

As it topples in the direction of the stairwell, its hard skull strikes the wooden railing. The unsettling noise of the dense bone fracturing prompts Chloe to pivot and look.

Pinching the surrounding air like a crab underwater, the creature tries one last time to grab something to thwart its fall, and, securing no handhold, it tumbles like a rag doll, end over end, down the entire flight of oak stairs.

As Chloe hears the final thud of the body impacting the last step, she realizes the music has stopped.

Timidly moving her legs to the top step, she glances over the railing to look at the gruesome aftermath of the Monster's brutal descent. What she sees on the floor below brings a smirk to her lips, knowing her intuition was correct. She watches with satisfaction as her mother's mangled body slowly morphs back into its original form as the Living Room Monster.

Slaying the creature that had pretended to be her mother makes her proud. "I'm not afraid of monsters," she says.

Standing in silence, she continues to look down upon the creature's body to assure it is dead. Content with the time she has taken to observe for signs of life and seeing none, she exhales a sigh of relief, and coming to terms with the demise of her tormentor, the weight of the world lifts from her shoulders.

She releases a giant yawn and reaches up to her face to rub her eyes. With her mind finally at peace and able to relinquish its defensive state, she realizes how far she has stayed awake past her bedtime. Staggering toward her room, her legs are barely able to carry her to the end of the hallway.

As she passes by the bathroom door, her exhaustion outweighs the immense amount of trauma that she had just encountered inside. Swiveling around to face her bedroom, she blankly stares at the wooden door and senses she has forgotten something.

From her peripheral vision, she glimpses the colorful sheen of speckling light that hits the floor through the stained-glass window. She turns her weary body to look at the beautiful color variations and notices several stray beams that illuminate a sign taped to the door next to hers. The dancing rays make her eyes wide with excitement. Walking in the direction of the door, she smiles as she reads the sign taped to the painted wood.

"Tim!" she states with a genuine giggle. Rushing toward her brother's room, she uses her finger to trace the sign of the crayon tractor drawing and smiles.

"Timothy," she says with an endearing smile.

Watching each ray of light dance across the picture elicits calmness to fall upon her. "I've found you," she says.

She immediately becomes torn by her emotions, placing her hand on the cold doorknob. Even though she is confident her brother is sleeping peacefully in his car-shaped bed, she still wants to check on him to ease her mind from any residual worry.

Not wanting to wake him, she ensures that she is extra quiet while opening his door. Slowly cracking it open, she notices that all the lights are off except for one. As she peeks her head inside of the room, her attention moves to a small nightlight that projects blurred outlines of moving dinosaurs across the walls.

When her mother goes missing at night, she is tasked with tucking her brother in, and due to his fear of darkness, she knows that he cannot sleep without it. Watching the images of the prehistoric creatures gives her a mental confirmation that he is safely asleep. The comfort provided by the enormous shadow of a Tyrannus Saurus gives her the courage to approach the small car-shaped bed sitting in the adjacent corner.

She steps closer and notices the covers are pulled up over a small mound, and the sight of a child's sleeping body causes her eyes to well with tears. "I told you everything would be okay," she whispers.

Lowering herself to the ground, her body faces the bed as she takes a seat on the floor. "You will always be safe, I promise," she says.

As she forms a fist with her right hand, her eyes intercept a harsh ray of light from a passing dinosaur, and sticking her little finger out; she kisses her thumb. "Cross my heart and hope to die. I pinkie swear," she whispers with a smile.

Overwhelmed by the blanket of fatigue that engulfs her body, she forces herself to stand groggily to her feet. "All I know is that things are going to be better now that I've found you," she says with a yawn.

Tiptoeing to the bedroom door, she takes a quick pause to look one last time at her peaceful brother. "Sweet dreams, Timothy. I love you," she says.

The thought of seeing her brother in the morning makes her smile as she quietly exits. Softly shutting the door behind her, she takes a moment to look at the stained-glass window and admire the brighter shades of orange that the rising sun has added to the mix of colors. The tranquility of the hallway fills her mind as she turns her body to face the direction of her room. She meanders to its entrance, feeling like she is floating on cloud nine as the sheer ecstasy of being at peace warms her soul.

Reaching her bedroom door, she sees the sign that reads NO BOYS ALLOWED and snickers. She remembers when she had naively painted the notice to keep her father away and how, just like every other attempt, it had failed.

Shrugging her shoulders, her eyes roll as she forces herself to open the door.

She walks with purpose as she enters her room and picks up the empty picture frame that sits on the nightstand next to her bed. Reaching into her pajama pocket, she pulls out the crumpled photo of Timothy's birthday and forces it back in the frame.

"I'm not afraid of you," she says, glaring at her mother in the photo as her hands place it back in its original spot next to her bed. Taking one last look at the image, she giggles. "I'm not afraid," she says.

Peeling back the top layer of covers, she climbs under the bed's sheets and turns off the lamp on her nightstand. The pure darkness created by the closed window shades unwinds her chaotic mind as she falls deeper into sleep.

And, for the first time, she experiences contentment.

Chapter Eleven

THEY CAN'T HURT US

Unwelcome light squeezes through each thin crack between the windows blinds. The glowing aura sheds truth on something peculiar within Chloe's childhood room. With the covers pulled to the top of her head, the only skin showing is the upper half of her forehead. Sunlight brushes across the tiny folds of her obscured complexion, causing each idiosyncrasy in her skin to be brought to life. Her exposed flesh shows signs of sweat, and each of her breaths becomes heavier than the last.

Her body, plagued by a horrible nightmare, induces her to toss and turn violently in her sleep. Her flailing hands hit the inside of her covers as if fighting something furious, making it impossible for her faded flowered sheets to continue to conceal her. Swinging her arms more aggressively than before, her propensity toward sleepwalking escalates as she mumbles incoherently. "I'm not afraid of you," she says.

Her feet join in the fight and rambunctiously kick underneath the sheets. She continues to toss and turn from the horrible dream, and her body's movements become more volatile. "I'm not afraid of monsters," she mumbles.

As her limbs thrash to fight the invisible demons, her legs stretch to their full length, and she stubs her toe on the footboard. "I'm not afraid!" she screams.

Her eyes jolt open from the pain, and she quickly realizes that she is too big for the bed. Laying without a top sheet reveals her true physical maturity. Still dressed in the same pink pajamas she had worn the night before, the petite frame of her forty-six-year-old body is similar in stature to her mother's, which makes the pajamas a much better fit than she recalled.

While listening to the sounds of the morning birds chirping outside, her breathing slows down to a manageable pace, and her anxiety lessens. Disoriented, she scans the room frantically to familiarize herself with her surroundings. It is not the usual one she sleeps in.

After practicing a breathing exercise, she calms herself further and remembers staying in her childhood room. Her dreams had felt so vivid that she had forgotten what reality is and is not. She had been determined never to come back home once she was old enough to leave and, for a moment, could not recall why she had returned in the first place.

Shuddering at the thought of the horrible nightmares, she cups her hands over her eyes to mitigate the repercussions of her post-traumatic stress. She blames a combination of her tumultuous childhood and the bedroom stay for the terrifying dream sequence. The prison walls that encapsulated her abusive childhood still haunt her, and she is disturbed by her involvement.

As she sits up in her bed, her toes stretch between the railings of the twin-size frame to ease an oncoming calf cramp. Looking past her wiggling toes, she notices the familiar duffel bag from her dream sitting open on the floor at the foot of the bed.

Frantically, she scrambles back toward the headboard as she senses the dream returning to haunt her. Shoved against the wood, her body silently faces the bag to analyze the vast similarities. An airline bag tag tied to the worn handle brings back a memory of boarding a plane to surprise her elderly parents for their fiftieth wedding anniversary. Along with the recollection, the countless complimentary cocktails consumed on her long flight fill the space between her eyes with an ache.

"I thought my psychiatrist said this was supposed to be therapeutic... the only thing I feel right now is shit," she says.

Using her two fingers to place pressure between her eyebrows, she gives her head a circling massage. Hungover, she closes her eyelids and stops the spinning room with a breathing exercise. Feeling that it has taken the edge off her anxiety, she opens her eyes and refocuses her gaze on the open duffel.

She scoots her body to the edge of the bed, places both feet onto the cold hardwood floor, lifts herself to a standing position, then anxiously inches her body toward the end of the bed. It terrifies her to look at the clothing protruding through the open zipper of the duffle, worried about seeing the soiled dress that haunted her childhood. Analyzing the contents at arm's length, she sees that everything is adult-sized, which calms her nerves.

As she moves closer towards the dingy bag, she reads the identification tag attached to the handle, and the information listed makes her chuckle as it details her maiden name. Having not returned home in twenty-eight years, she could not help but think of the irony in the timing of her divorce and how her names reversal had taken place not long before her trip. She cringes at the fact that she is one of the family again. "Fucking cliche," she mutters.

Not wanting to look at her name, she rips off the tag, crumples it, and throws it deep into the bag. She rummages around inside the duffel until she locates the bottle of prescription pills for her anxiety and shakes a couple into her hand. Adding a little ibuprofen to the mix to combat her headache, she tosses the pill cocktail down her dry throat.

As she rolls her eyes to mask the pain, she strolls to the window and opens the blinds, and the light flooding the room makes her wince. She releases a yawn as her eyes adjust to the brightness. Stretching her body to the sky and now feeling a bit soberer, she turns around to scan the layout of the old familiar room.

Making her way back towards her bed, her view becomes distracted by the nightstand. Redirecting her trajectory to the small piece of furniture, she checks for a detail she remembers from her dream. She releases a large exhalation, relieved to see the framed photo of Timothy's birthday missing from her nightstand. Thinking it odd how vivid her memory is about aspects of previous events, she worries that her anxiety may be worsening and returns to her bag to grab the bottle of pills.

Placing the container in the pocket of her pajamas, she redirects her attention to the door. Without allowing another moment to conjure more of her horrific memories, she exits the room and does not look back.

As she steps into the hallway, she pauses to look at the closed bathroom door across from her. Unable to control her trembling, she forces her lungs to take a deep breath as she shakes her head in disbelief at her body's reaction to the sight of the door. "Get over yourself," she states.

Walking to the restroom, she cautiously opens the door to let herself inside, and, refusing to look at the bathtub, she makes her way to the sink as she giggles anxiously.

Covering the sides of her eyes as if wearing horse blinders, she sprints to the vanity mirror mounted above the sink. Unmindful of her surroundings, Chloe inadvertently kicks something with her foot. Hearing plastic skid across the tile floor prompts her to look down at her feet, and immediately, she notices a child's stool. It is the same one she had used in her dream.

The stool's momentum fueling carries it next to the shelving under the sink. Uneasy with the stool's familiarity, Chloe is frightened to check the tub, and with tunnel vision, she shifts her pupils to focus on her reflection in the mirror.

Even though her appearance looks disheveled, the normalcy of her middle-aged stature calms her. Making eye contact with her reflection, she cannot help but laugh at the ridiculous notion that her dreams can trigger a fear response that is so debilitating.

She tries to distract her mind by counting the tiling on the floor that surrounds her tapping feet, but as she reaches the tenth tile, she spots her childhood princess toothbrush lying on the ground by the side of the sink, and the sight of it opens the floodgates of fear in her mind.

Trying to knock herself out of her cycle of having another panic attack, she reaches in her pocket to retrieve her anxiety medication. "Why isn't it working?" she says. Fumbling with the bottle, she accidentally drops the canister onto the floor and watches as it rolls next to the toothbrush. Seeing the two items collide makes her breathing grow shallow, her heart race, and hyperventilation ensues.

Amid a panic attack, she knows she must retrieve her prescription and forces herself to bend down. As she lowers herself to the floor to pick up her pill bottle, the urge for a fix overcomes her, causing her to forget about her worries regarding the tub, and she unintentionally spots its outline in her peripherals.

Her right forearm quivers as it stretches to fetch the medication. Readjusting her left palm, which is gripping the tile for better support, her knuckle slides on a slippery substance, and she panics. Before taking hold of her pills, the momentum from the loss of traction causes her arms to give out from under her.

Upon impact with the frigid tile floor, she experiences a moment of unconsciousness. Taking a minute to gather her bearings, she rolls herself onto her side to see what she has slipped on, and her eyes stop dead on the substance.

A large darkened-red smudge contaminates the white tile, and remnants of small clots fester in the adjoining cream-colored grouted joints. Still fuzzy from the fall, she manically rubs her eyes to improve her vision, hopeful that her mind is just playing tricks on her. Lowering her fists from her face, she sees her hand-stained crimson red. Frozen, in disbelief, her eyes scan the floor for the culprit, and to her horror, realizes that it is not a hallucination. The puddle is indeed blood.

Her racing mind sends tremors down her spine. As her gaze follows the trail of bodily fluid, she notices the stream getting denser. At the scarlet river's end lies a thick piece of skin with a torn, weathered appearance. Something snaps inside of her, and she becomes numb to the situation.

Detaching herself makes her embody her childlike character again, and she boosts herself up to crawl on all fours. As she looks at her hands, she can see her youth has been restored. The sleeves of her pajamas drag against the ground and cushion her crawling palms.

Locking her curiosity on the severed piece of skin a short distance away, she inches herself closer, and her hands carefully pick it up to inspect it. Her adult anxiety is replaced by calm with each curious scan of her eye.

As she holds the skin closer to her pupil, she notices that there are nostril holes, along with a piece of broken cartilage. In her mind, she has solved the mystery of the strange flesh. It is a nose. The pride in her discovery makes her lips quiver with excitement.

"But who do you belong to?" she quietly asks. Holding the disfigured organ up to her eye, she spins herself around to look for the owner, giggling as her gaze fixates on the bathtub.

A lifeless arm with battered skin dangles over the porcelains edge, and attached to the limp appendage is the corpse of her elderly father. Wearing the same outfit like the one in her dream, his body is dressed in an old suit with tails and a white shirt aged with a tinge of yellow. As he lays calmly reclined in the water, she can see his bowler hat floating next to him like a toy sailboat. His open eyes are bulged and bloodshot from being strangled. The skin on his face appears more coriaceous than when she saw him last, almost three decades ago. Mismatched from his face, his jaw sits crooked, with a protruding tongue that his misfitting dentures have half amputated.

Finding similarities to the gruesome scene from the night before, her mind is unfazed by the image. "Karma's a bitch, isn't it?" she says.

Looking in between his protruding eyes and misaligned jaw, she notices a hole where his nose should be. "Eureka," she excitedly states.

Her gape freezes on the tub scene, she closes her left eyelid, and, extending the nose out in front of her open right eye, she squints to see if the proportion of the nostrils aligns with the body. Upon completing her analysis, she confidently determines that it belongs to her father. "Who's the tough one now?" she asks.

Rising to her feet, she notices a dust bunny on the nose's tip and polishes it off on her pajamas. Leisurely, she walks over to the tub to hover above the corpse. As she looks at the string that cuts through her father's neck, she distinguishes something that differs from before: unlike in the dream, the elastic band decapitating him still has the red clown nose attached.

Bending down over the body, she snatches the red ball between her fingers to squeak it and watches his neck wound deepen as she pulls the object towards her. As she tries to free the nose from its string, the surrounding water turns a darker hue of red. After several forceful tugs, she successfully plucks the ball from its cord, like a cherry from a stem, and the momentum causes her to fall on the ground.

She waves both noses in the air as she sits on the floor. "I got your nose," she says with a laugh.

Rising to her feet, she walks back to the tub and places the severed skin over the hole like a missing puzzle piece. "I'm not a monster," she says with a smirk.

As she squeaks the ball one last time, her fingers hold it to the sky. "Don't you worry. I'll take good care of it," she says with a wink. The red spongy ball releases one last squeak as she wrings it out over the tub before placing it in her pocket.

Knowing that the clown nose will never again prompt trauma-filled events makes her feel satisfied. As she turns around to the sink, she scans the floor to find the princess' toothbrush and sees it still lying next to her bottle of pills on the floor. Coasting at a leisurely pace, her body meanders over to her items. As she picks them up, she takes a moment to look at the prescription in her hand. She pops open the bottle and walks to the vanity. "Some child-proof lock this is," she says.

With her hands full, she reaches the side of her foot to the small stool next to the sink and ushers it to the front of the bowl so she can stand on it. As she climbs on top, she turns the faucet on hot and empties the contents of the prescription bottle into the porcelain basin. Watching each pill fall down the drain brings her joy, and the steam from the boiling water soothes her. Her hand wraps tighter around the toothbrush and, holding the bristles in the faucet's direction, she dips the toothbrush under the water and begins compulsively brushing her teeth.

The sight of her bleeding gums corroborates that she has finished. Setting the toothbrush on the counter, Chloe continues with her morning routine. "It's just another day," she mumbles.

As she moves her hands through the scalding water, she immediately retracts them with a wince. Shrugging off the extreme temperature, she forces her hands back under the running faucet to clean her face. She finishes washing the leftover blood from rubbing her eyes and turns off the spigot. Picking up the toothbrush from the counter, she shoves the sticky end into her pocket along with the clown nose.

Her eyes shift back to the bathtub as she dries her hands on her pajamas. Disgusted by her father's aged appearance, she rolls her eyes as she exits the bathroom and shuts the door behind her.

As she makes her way to the staircase, an epiphany occurs within her brain. Thinking that she could be dreaming makes her feet pirouette, and the uncaring nature of her childish body makes her fine with the outcome as long as the monsters are gone.

Her hand swiftly grabs for the railing, and the sensation of something slippery makes her jump. Raising her fingers to her gaze, she analyzes the skin and notices the same red substance from the bathroom clings to her extremity. Chloe takes a closer look and sees that the gore has blended into the cracks of the dark-washed wood, giving it cherry accents.

Curious about the crimson varnish, her eyes follow each groove of the wooden railing to the floor below, and the glorious memories encapsulated within her dream flood her mind. Peering down to the end of the scarlet trail, her glance is met by her mother's mangled body. Seeing that she looks different in the daylight interests her, and she makes a descent down the steps to get a better look.

Halfway to the bottom, she stops and, with a clearer view of her mother's face, quickly takes notice of her aged features and wrinkled appearance. The familiarity of seeing the same all-black attire from the night before on her body brings warmth to her bones. She taps her head as she connects the dots regarding her parents' outfits color-coordinating with each other and rules out her preconceived idea that her mother was in a state of mourning. Knowing she was devoid of sadness before perishing eliminates any guilt from Chloe's psyche.

Taking a couple of steps closer, she notices shards of shattered glass surrounding her mother, and, dodging the stray pieces, she steps nearer. As she stoops over the corpse, her mind refuses to believe that the body is real. With her big toe, she probes the fractured pieces of her mother's spine piercing through the skin on her neck. The perfect placement of each bone looks like a special effect crafted by a prop master for a movie. She gazes at the top of the stairs to visualize its distance to make the gruesome scene.

No longer entertained by the bone, she investigates to see where the shattered glass has come from. Spotting a more significant piece with a partial label excites her. As she picks it up to read the writing, it becomes immediately evident that the broken bottle belongs to her favorite whiskey." I always knew that the bottle was going to kill you, one way or another," she sarcastically says.

Her mother's dress is hiked up on one side, revealing a large gash on her thigh. Thinking of the memory in the dining room rouses Chloe to chuckle. Even though she did not inflict the wound, she is impressed by the series of events that realistically led to it.

When thinking of the odds involved in her falling on top of her whiskey bottle's knifelike glass shards, her eyes widen with disbelief. It was evident to her that her mother's alcoholism had caused her demise, and for that reason, she exudes disgust rather than sympathy.

As she steps over the twisted body, she casually shrugs. "Can't help everyone," she says.

Enthusiastic about having the downstairs to herself, she speeds up her walking pace as she traverses the room to the record player. She turns it on and adjusts the needle onto the vinyl. Her ears remember the sound of the music being played repeatedly from the single record that she now has control of. Thinking of the maltreatment that the simple piece of plastic introduced throughout her treacherous childhood infuriates her.

She cringes at the scratching needle as she anticipates that the familiarly haunting melody will soon play. Confusion overrides her emotion when a different song resonates from the same album. This one brings happiness and a smile to her face. Merrily humming along with the tune of the melody, her jubilant demeanor emanates an air of being born again. In her opioid-induced state, she trots to the left and opens her mother's alcohol cabinet, aggressively grabbing for an unopened bottle of whiskey.

"Considering that we have been through hell and back, this one's for you, darlin,'" she states.

Her body turns to face her mother as if she is about to give a reception speech. Raising the bottle to the sky, she points the corked end toward her corpse. "Looks like I'm still here," she says with a laugh. Plucking the tightly wedged plug away from the top of the bottle, she takes three large gulps. As she senses a droplet of liquid dripping down her chin, she grabs a handful of her pink pajamas to clean it.

"That was one hell of a fucking toast, huh, mommy?" she shouts across the room. Chloe continues glaring at her mother's corpse and sees a fly land on her open eye, and the sight makes her neurotically laugh. "It's been one HELL of a ride."

She rolls her eyes as she takes another chug from the bottle of whiskey. She extends her second and third digits, and in an, I see you gesture, she points at her eyes than to those of her mother. "Monkey sees, monkey do," she says. As she clutches the bottle tighter, her grip forces her throat to take another sip.

Still fueled by years of pent-up anger, she shifts her plan of action to distract herself. Quickly redirecting her energy, her legs walk thru the dining room and towards the kitchen. She sings as she joyously dances to the beat. As she enters the chaos-free kitchen, she cannot help cheering. "Can't a woman get a cup of coffee in this place?" she asks while laughing.

Mid-spin, she darts her pointer finger to hit the brew button on the coffee machine. Setting the open bottle of whiskey next to the coffee maker, she turns around to the cupboard to grab a mug. A coffee cup with the phrase #1 DAD catches her attention. Grabbing it off the shelf, she looks at it with skepticism. "I sure as hell didn't buy this one," she says.

The sound of the coffee maker beeping behind her stops her rambling thoughts, and she turns around with the ironic mug. She walks towards the coffee maker with a cup in hand

and pours herself a coffee–alcohol blend; as she sips on the warm liquid, her stomach growls. She scans the kitchen counter for food to eat and remembers the cupcakes. The sight of the perfectly packaged, blue-frosted cakes she brought as a celebratory gift for her parents fills her with happiness.

As she approaches the ornate packaging, her mouth waters. The premier wrapping is near perfect. Someone opened just a single corner to accommodate the removal of two delectable treats the prior evening. Her gaze takes notice of the small note attached to the bow, and she snatches it up to read it aloud.

"Happy fiftieth anniversary," she states with a snicker.

At once, her parents' matching black-tie attire makes sense to her as she recounts the image of her mother's dress. "I mean, not my first choice for a date night, but whatever floats your boat," she says.

As she finishes aggressively crumpling the handwritten note into a tight ball, she pretends to play basketball with it and throws it into the sink's disposal. Her fingers lunge for the grinder's switch above the countertop, and as she flips it on, she notices something shiny in the sink and moves closer to get a better look. The presence of the infamous butcher knife fills her with excitement. She grabs the weapon by the handle and, using the same hand, turns on the sink to wash it. After securing the knife inside the elastic band of pants, she listens to the deeply fulfilling sound of the grinder's blades eating the papyrus.

Her claws grab the open bottle of whiskey, and she pours a generous amount into her mug. "Yuck, cooties," she says with a chuckle.

As she places the whiskey back on the counter, she gets a glimpse of the fridge, and the humming makes her shudder. "What are you looking at?" she angrily shouts. Not receiving a response from the appliance sparks her annoyance, and she rolls her eyes.

Her hunger kicks into overdrive, and, seeing that the only food in the house is her gifted cupcakes, she grabs one. Breaking off the frosted end, she keeps the chocolate base and tosses the blue-painted portion into the swirling disposal. She opens the fridge to search for other options and, finding none, takes a bite. Hating the taste, she quickly spits it out onto the floor and shoves the remaining part of the cupcake back into the packaging. "Glad they liked it better than me," she says.

As she leans the weight of her body against the counter, she relaxes, inhaling the aroma of coffee and cake. The combination of smells reminds her of the holidays. Taking a moment to savor the reminiscence, she closes her eyes. "It's a new day; you just have to breathe," she whispers like a mantra.

Taking in another deep breath, she falls into a profound state of meditation and, rejuvenated, walks towards the living room with her coffee in hand. The music grows louder with her approach, triggering her free movements across the living room.

While dancing around the space, she hums a melodic tune. Mid-spin, she sips on her coffee, stopping only for a moment to stare at a significant "Happy Anniversary!" floral arrangement sitting on the coffee table. Without breaking eye contact with the object, her feet walk like a brain-dead zombie towards the ghastly homage.

Her mind on autopilot, she reaches for the colorful arrangement of red roses and sneers. Plucking a single rose from the bunch, she screams as she throws it at her mother's corpse. "Fuck you, you piece of shit!" she yells. As she calmly returns to drinking her coffee, her finger proceeds to trace each petal of the bouquet as if painting a picture.

Becoming more intoxicated, her words begin to slur, followed by uncontrollable laughter. After chugging the rest of her spiked drink, her body turns to look at her mother's corpse. She chuckles at each of the horrible memories that pop into her mind from her childhood. "Now you finally know how it feels!" she shouts.

Her arm throws the empty coffee cup against the wall. As she claps at the harsh sound of the cup breaking, she notices the basement door, and her brother comes to mind. "Timothy," she whispers.

Remembering that he is still peacefully sleeping in his room brings her a sense of joyful happiness. Quickly moving across the living room, her feet gingerly hop over her mother, and she begins zigzagging her way up the staircase.

Halfway up the stairs, she stops to look at the progression of family photos lining the wall. She stares with confusion at the spot that previously housed the picture of them playing in the leaves. The contents within the frame have been replaced with Timothy's birthday party photo from her nightstand.

As she steps closer, she realizes the image's paper is crinkled. Chloe looks to the next photo leading up the staircase, it is a family portrait, and her brother is missing from the picture. The birthday photo is his last recorded image in the procession. Not wanting to deal with feelings of sadness, she glances towards his room and ascends the rest of the stairs.

Barely hanging on his door by a small, discolored piece of tape is an old sheet of construction paper with a hand-drawn picture of a tractor. Standing on the top step, her eyes glance over at the sign, which has not been touched in forty-odd years.

Unable to contain her excitement any longer, she rushes down the hallway and opens Timothy's door. The room is identical to when she had checked on him the night before. Even the dinosaur light still brightly swirls Jurassic images. On his nightstand is a photo of them playing in the leaves together, and next to it is his inhaler.

She notices his tiny body under the covers and tiptoes to his side. Reaching underneath the bed, she pulls out his collection of marbles. Lightly touching his comforter, she says, "I know I haven't been around for a while... I'm sorry I've missed so many birthdays."

Her hand reaches into her pocket and pulls out the clown's nose. "I brought you a marble," she says with a smile.

Still trying not to wake him, she places the red nose inside the box with the rest of his marble collection, then stands up and carefully grabs the photo from his nightstand. Not wanting her younger brother to see her cry, she hastily exits the room. Before closing the door, she peeks inside one last time.

"Love you, Tim. Night," she says while quietly closing the door.

She clutches the framed photo tighter in her arms and, holding back her tears; she makes her way to her room.

Letting herself inside, she rushes to the open duffel bag and empties her pockets. She places the knife into the bag, carefully lays the picture frame on top, and zips it shut. Then, placing the strap over her shoulder, her posture straightens as her feet carry her downstairs.

Stopping as she reaches the doorway, she turns to look at the record player. She sprints to the turntable without a second thought and seizes the album mid-spin. Raising it to the ceiling to identify the artist, she realizes it is an unlabeled vinyl.

Knowing that her departure is time-sensitive, she picks up her pace. As she heads toward the exit, her eyes cannot help but fixate on the welding apron hanging next to the basement door. She briefly reroutes her path. Standing in front of the apron, she reaches her hand inside to find the skeleton key and locks the basement door.

Chloe sets her bag on the floor, unzips it, and places the record and key inside. As she prepares to zip her duffle, she momentarily freezes when her eyes catch a final glimpse of the green welding apron. With one last shudder, she springs to her feet, dashes to the object, and rips it from its nail. As she finishes stuffing the bulky apron inside her duffle, her fingers give the zipper one last tug. Her shoulder lifts the bag by the strap, and she runs for the exit.

Placing her hand on the door evokes her body to experience temporary paralysis, and a cold surge of prickling pinches traverses her skin as she turns the knob.

Endeavoring to forget the past, she exits and shuts the door.

ABOUT AUTHOR

Gitte Tamar

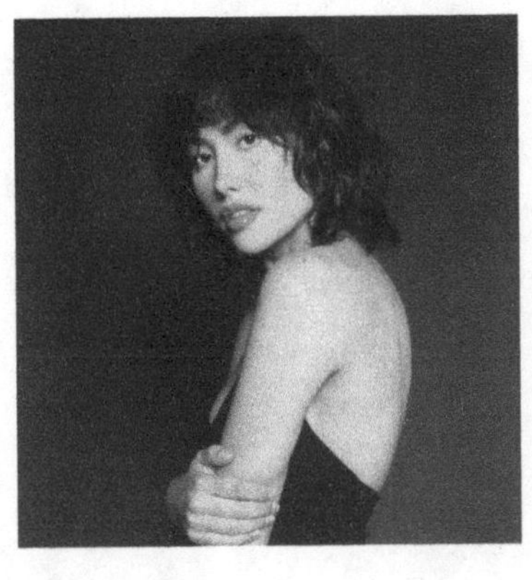

Brigitte, "Gitte," Tamar was born in a small rural Oregon town. Growing up, she was enthralled by scary tales featuring poetic tones and consistently gravitated towards writing darkened narratives. In *Run, Run, Baby,* Brigitte explores past trauma's effects on mental health in the format of a psychological thriller. *Run, Run, Baby* is Brigitte's second commercial horror novel.